CUPIDS AND CORONETS

Lady Caroline Eaton works for her father, the Earl of Thornbury, in their stately home as a guide. When Magnus Manisty, an American tourist, falls in love with her Caroline tells him she is engaged to her friend Richard Verney. Magnus begins to believe that there is an unbridgeable gap between them. Yet, Richard is not the paragon Caroline believes him to be, and pride prevents her from acknowledging her feelings. But Magnus is a charming and persuasive suitor . . .

CHARLES STUART

CUPIDS AND CORONETS

Complete and Unabridged

LINFORD
Leicester

First published in Great Britain in 1974 by
Robert Hale Limited
London

First Linford Edition
published 2008
by arrangement with
Robert Hale Limited
London

British Library CIP Data

Stuart, Charles, *1924* –
    Cupids and coronets.—Large print ed.—
Linford romance library
    1. Love stories
    2. Large type books
    I. Title
    823.9′14 [F]

    ISBN 978–1–84782–341–0

Published by
F. A. Thorpe (Publishing)
Anstey, Leicestershire

Set by Words & Graphics Ltd.
Anstey, Leicestershire
Printed and bound in Great Britain by
T. J. International Ltd., Padstow, Cornwall

This book is printed on acid-free paper

For Ellis Amburn

1

Caroline stood and watched the people milling about in the drive and the garden. Somehow she enjoyed this, although in the beginning she had hated the intrusion. One could not help having a slightly smug feeling when all these people came to admire one's home. They weren't all peasants either, or anarchists making notes on what to burn down come the revolution. There were Jags and Rovers in the car park, which had once been the tennis courts.

'Plenty of parking space and lots of lavatories,' Bertram Batty, the family solicitor, had advised them when they first decided to get into the Stately Home Stakes. He had been right too. Both were essential.

She felt pangs of guilt as she stood there in the early June sunlight, a pretty girl, tall and lissome with a head of beautiful white-gold hair. She did not merely stand out in a crowd — she dazzled the beholder; if you happened to like blondes, that is. She really ought to be helping Aunt Selina and Mr. Cook today, acting as a guide. This could be quite fun, and she often got tips which she pocketed gleefully. Americans sometimes gave her 50p or even a pound. After a good weekend she frequently went up to town to do some shopping, and have lunch at The Royal Garden Hotel in Kensington, all on tips.

She was about to turn and go back inside the house when she saw the man staring at her. She stared back, curious. He was tall and broad shouldered, with thick, bleached hair, and a good tan. Where had he got the tan, she wondered? The weather hadn't been all that good. Perhaps he was an American, fresh from Florida, with a pocket full of 50p pieces. He came towards her, taking long easy strides. Not an American, she thought. The clothes were English; English and good quality. He probably shopped in Jermyn Street, and drove a Mercedes 230 SL convertible with automatic transmission and power steering.

'Excuse me,' he said politely and she blinked. He *was* American, too. No doubt about it.

'Yes.'

'Haven't I met you before?'

She made a face. 'Can't you do better than that?' she asked. 'You know you haven't.'

'Oh.' Her forthright rejection floored him. 'Well then, why haven't we met before?'

'Probably because I haven't come over here on a trip from America. I live in this country.'

'So do I,' he grinned. 'For the past three years. Come and have tea. It's probably ghastly, but it is something to do.'

'The tea is very good,' she contradicted briskly. 'It is excellent in fact, and the scones are fresh daily, and the butter is real butter, farmhouse butter.'

'Sorry.' He laughed. 'Obviously you've been here before. Don't tell me you've already had tea.'

'No . . .'

'Good. That's great. We can have tea together. My name is Magnus Manisty.'

'What?'

'I assure you it is.'

'I'm Caroline. Where did you get the name?'

'I believe from the Orkneys. My grandfather was an Orcadian anyway. Beyond that I don't know. We Manistys are a mystery. I bought a dictionary of surnames once but mine wasn't listed. I prefer it that way. I can make up my own story whenever I want, and who can contradict me?'

'That must be very useful in America.'

'Do I detect a slight note of disparagement? I hope not.'

'I'm sorry, I didn't mean to be nasty. Let's sit over there in the corner. It's rather a pleasant spot.'

'Good. I see they have table service. That's something. Do you come here often?'

'I live locally,' she replied evasively.

'I like it here too. I have a flat in Richmond, which isn't too far away. For some reason or another, I haven't come here before.'

'You live at Richmond and you haven't been to Walton?'

'No, never. Anyway I've only been at Richmond a year. Before that I spent two years in West Ken, which wasn't too much fun. Flats are difficult in and around London.'

'I suppose so. What do you do?'

He leaned closer and grinned again, a frank, engaging sort of smile which she decided she liked. 'I work for a publisher. This is what you call a busman's holiday.'

'I don't follow you.'

A waitress came up to take the order, gave Caroline a startled look and received a warning frown in return. She left full of the news that Lady Caroline was having tea with one of the visitors.

'Now,' Magnus said returning to the subject. 'Where was I? Oh yes. I've just been given the English Heritage Series to edit. That's a sort of promotion. We're very proud of that series. It includes the Starr Guide to England's Stately Homes, which at £10.50 is guaranteed to enhance the most elegant coffee tables. I've decided to check up on some of these stately homes for myself. It sounds like an awful racket to me. This one is near to where I live, so here I am, checking up.'

'You have an exposé in mind?' she asked mildly.

'No, this is just for personal amusement. In the offices of Laker & Day, bespoke publishers to the carriage trade, we speak of stately homes with cringing respect. This place not only keeps some doddering Colonel Blimp in cigars and port, which he has done nothing to deserve, but it also keeps me alive too — and everyone else in Laker & Day. The English Heritage Series of which I am now proud editor not only provides much bread and butter for all, but even jam, and sometimes wine to wash it all down.'

Caroline was watching him as he talked. He spoke animatedly and with a sense of gaiety. He obviously enjoyed life. It was a bit of a coincidence him working for Laker & Day and being editor of the series which included their magnificent volume on stately homes. There were some excellent photographs of her own home in it.

Tea was served. Caroline poured and they helped themselves to fresh scones with pale gold butter and an assortment of jams and honey.

'Not at all bad,' Magnus said approvingly when he had sipped tea. 'I've studied this tea business pretty thoroughly. I reckon I can make as good a cup of tea as any Englishman. This is okay. Of course at 50p for a set tea, it darned well ought to be.'

'There's no profit in it, or not much, not when there are all the staff to pay.'

'How do you know?'

She bit her lip. 'It's obvious, isn't it?'

'There must be profit in something. They don't invite the general public to trample all over their gardens just for the fun of it, do they? Of course there's the entrance, which must be all profit. It isn't cheap — 20p to get past the gate and another 20p to get into the house.'

'Last year it was 15,' she told him, concealing her amusement. 'You left it too late.'

'Just my luck. Then there's another 30p for a brochure, which from what I saw of it, is little more than a broadsheet. That *is* a racket; and I speak as one who is in the racket, so to speak.'

'You can have it autographed free,' she pointed out.

'By whom? Bing Crosby? Doris Day? President Nixon? No, by some crusty old peer nobody has ever heard of. I don't even know his name.'

'The 7th Earl of Thornbury.'

'I see you have read the publicity

handout. Is yours autographed?'

She shook her head, delighted at the fun of it all. Why should she get her father to autograph one of his own booklets for her?

'I smell a fellow republican.'

'I am not,' she contradicted sharply.

'I apologise. Let's finish the arithmetic. There is a maze for which they charge 10p extra. I reckon they must average at least a pound a head. Call it only 80p to be on the safe side. It's a racket all right.'

'What about their expenses? People damage property, you know, and there are guides, staff to provide the teas, gardeners to clear up the mess. It's not all profit. I wonder what it actually cost to produce *your* book on stately homes? The cost to the publisher I mean. About four pounds I'd say. It sells at over ten pounds.'

'You know,' he told her expansively, 'this is exactly what I don't understand about you English. You seem to be even more impressed by your decadent aristocracy than we poor foreigners are. One would think that you, at least, would see through them; but no, you love them. Didn't someone say that every Englishman loves a Lord?'

'I'm sure they did,' Caroline answered abruptly, not enjoying the day so much. 'Like most successful nations we've had just about everything said about us.'

'Prickly, aren't you?' He laughed. 'I didn't mean to annoy you Caroline. Tell me about yourself. Where do you live?'

'Here in Walton.'

'You don't say. Imagine that. I'm surprised you don't go further afield than this for your amusement. How come that there is no boyfriend lurking in the bushes?'

'I'm meeting him in half an hour.'

'I might have guessed it. I was about to invite you out for dinner.'

'I'm afraid that's out of the question.'

'Where do you work?'

'I don't, not really. I help at home.'

'In these days of Women's Lib? A kitchen serf? A galley slave?'

'Galley?'

'I use it in the culinary sense. It is a clever pun. A galley is where they cook on board ship. Galley slave. Get it?'

'Now that I've been hit over the head with it,' she agreed coolly.

'You disappoint me.'

'I can't think why. At least I'm not a publisher's lackey.'

'Owch, that really hurt. Have the last scone. I shall send for more, and blow the expense.'

'Don't order any more on my account.'

'I am thinking of my own account too,' he laughed. 'Stop being mysterious Caroline. Tell me, what does your father do?'

'This and that. Mostly nothing. Welfare state,' she added with a wink.

He stared at her. She was so lovely, so well-dressed, so much the sort of girl one would like to have living next door. She had that important educated accent which he had learned to look for among the English. Could her family really be living on a Government hand-out? It didn't seem likely.

'You're having me on.'

'A little. I really must go inside.'

'Such a hurry,' he complained, stopping a waitress and handing her a pound. 'All right. I'll come along too. I want to see this famous octagon room that has everyone ooh-ing and ah-ing; and the entrance hall. Maybe they are as good as the lovely colour illustrations in my book.'

'*Your* book? You didn't write it.'

'I spoke in the trade sense. I am now responsible for the sales of the thing, and for revising it and adding to it. What's your surname?'

'Eaton.'

'You have a nice name. I love your hair. I also love your freckles. Can't you ditch this boyfriend of yours?'

'He wouldn't like that.'

'Is he bigger than I am?'

'Smaller,' she replied.

'Ah,' he said with satisfaction.

'He's very tough,' she added.

'As long as he's really small I don't mind. Seriously, I must see you again.'

'I can't think why. Aren't there any girls in Richmond? Or up in town?'

'Millions. I'm not interested.'

'If that's flattery it's crude.'

'The truth is always crude,' he quipped.

'I must go.'

'I'm coming too.'

He walked beside her to the front door of the house. As she went inside he stopped and bought two tickets. When he caught up with her in the magnificent wooden panelled entrance hall with its gallery at the top of the stairs, running all round the first floor, she was turning to face an elderly, grey-haired woman.

'Caroline, where have you been darling?'

'Having tea, Aunt Selina.'

'So soon? Look darling, you'll have to take this lot. There are enough to start now. I'll be back for the next bunch.' She looked up at Magnus who was now standing at Caroline's shoulder. 'Oh hullo,' she greeted him vaguely. 'All right Caroline? You've got about fifteen here. You're welcome to them.'

'All right. See you later.'

As Aunt Selina hurried off Caroline moved away. Magnus grabbed her gently and held her.

'What is this?' he asked suspiciously. 'Do you *work* here?'

Her smile was sparkling. 'Sometimes.' She disengaged herself. 'I must take this bunch round, and that includes you Mr. Manisty. You've got a ticket haven't you?'

'Two.' He made a face. 'One for you.'

'You're very sweet. You can go round twice.'

She walked away. Magnus hesitated for a moment and then walked back to the elderly man in the shiny suit who was selling tickets.

'Hey, excuse me.'

The man looked up and smiled politely.

'The blonde called Caroline. Who is

she? Do you know?'

The man blinked. 'Certainly sir. That's Lady Caroline Eaton, Lord Thornbury's daughter. She's taking the party round now. I think you can catch up with them.'

'Oh boy,' Magnus said quietly to himself.

'Pardon?' the attendant asked.

'Nothing. Thanks a lot.'

He hurried back to the little throng of eager sightseers who had paid their 20p to see the interior of Portcullis Manor, Walton on Thames.

*   *   *

The *Starr Guide to England's Stately Homes*, written by the Hon. Vincent Starr, an impoverished scion of the nobility who had handsomely remedied his financial distress by writing about the upper classes and the homes they inhabited, devoted two pages, 18 and 19, to Portcullis Manor. There were some truly excellent colour illustrations, including one of the magnificent octagon room with its unique chandelier. There was also a lyrical blurb about this lovely Carolean manor house set like a jewel among acres of trees on the outskirts of Walton, beside the Thames. It possessed a splendid topiary garden which was famous, a fine maze for which there was an extra charge, a fabulous collection of antique furniture and furnishings, a truly lovely entrance hall and grand staircase — and the octagon room, that strange out-of-place feature of the house. Experts swore it was not a recent addition, and it was now believed that the room was used by Charles II who came to Portcullis Manor to meet the beautiful wife of the 9th Viscount Thornbury, with whom he had had a passionate love affair, so discreetly conducted that even now there were historians who said it was all bunkum. Certainly it was a fine house with notable plasterwork and moulded ceilings, but it was the octagon room which made all the difference between having, say, a mere ten thousand visitors a year and the actual figure of over thirty thousand. Seventeen miles from London, on a lovely part of the Thames, it attracted visitors as jam attracts wasps.

For ten years Portcullis Manor had been open to the public, and now it provided both an occupation and an income for the Eatons, including the aged Aunt Selina, as well as a sort of local industry. On early closing day, which was Wednesday, and on Saturday and Sunday, from the beginning of May till the end of October, people poured into the house and grounds, brandishing their money. The locals were on to a good thing, helping out for three pounds per head a day, and paid in cash too, at the end of each day. If one was keen, one could pick up an extra nine pounds a week, and there were no records, so what the income tax didn't know was really nobody's business.

It was not, however, quite the racket Magnus Manisty suspected it might be. The cost of running a three-century old manor house, with beautiful grounds which required several gardeners to keep them in order, was not inconsiderable. All the death duties had now been paid off, and money was being hoarded away; but this apparent profit was mainly to enable Caroline, the only child of her widowed father, to meet the insatiable demand of the Government when he died, without her having to sell the ancestral bed and breakfast. The truth was that they lived well and even elegantly, that there were two expensive cars in the garage, but that they had no real capital of their own — only a reserve fund for the future rapacious demands of an insatiable egalitarian Government.

As a way of life it was almost idyllic, if you did not object to being stared at and invaded three days a week, six months a year — nothing is without its price. At the moment Magnus was ignorant of all this. He was following Caroline from room to room, admiring the beauties of the house, and cursing at having made a fool of himself.

It was not his fault of course. He did not usually rush in and try to pick up pretty girls, not even when they had that lovely, fresh, freckled gorgeous blonde look which Caroline possessed. He had planned to make this visit with Lisette Taylor, another blonde, somewhat more streamlined as becomes a highly-paid and well-known photographic model. Lisette modelled clothes — never swim suits and never furs. She was against killing animals. She was important enough to dictate her own terms. The result was that she was a bit of a prima donna at times, and last night she and Magnus had had a truly splendid row, and had parted swearing never to meet again.

So, instead of going to Putney today to collect her and bring her to admire this minor stately home, he had gone off alone, had a snack at a country pub, and finally come to Portcullis, driven by sheer boredom. In other words, he was on the rebound, because he had admired Lisette Taylor enormously. It had seemed like a sign from above when, on the very day after the quarrel, he laid eyes on a girl even more attractive. He had not thought this possible.

He began to lose interest in the house, especially after they had seen the fabulous octagon room, all white and gilt, with enormous mirrors, and its truly astonishing gilded ceiling. Instead he stared frankly at Caroline. He was filled with admiration at the way she trotted out facts and figures, her calm manner when dealing with questions, many of them fatuous, and the way she seemed to grace each room. He could hardly wait till it was all over. At last they were back in the hall and people were leaving. He hurried over to Caroline.

'That was great. You're the perfect guide.'

'Thank you.' She was cool to the point of being icy.

'You must have thought me pretty brash.'

'Not unusually so.' The barriers were still up, but he did not care.

'When can I see you again — properly, I mean? Not here with all these people around.'

'I rather like these people. They pay.'

'Come off it Caroline. I want to talk to you. I want to find out all about the stately home business. I'm interested.'

'I don't give interviews.'

'I'm not some reporter,' he said hotly. 'I want to know about it. Is that so unreasonable?'

'Go and ask Bath or Bedford. They're in the First Division. We're only in the Second.'

He had been in England long enough to recognise the titles of English peers.

'Okay, so you're Second Division,' he shrugged. 'You can still tell me what I want to know. I'm not going to publish it, for heaven's sake.'

'I'm sorry but you'll have to talk to my father. It's his house.'

'Where is he?' Magnus asked automatically.

'If you go out through the side door there, you'll probably find him autographing brochures. Sometimes he does four hundred in a day, poor darling. I tell him he should charge extra for it. I know I would,' she added giving him a defiant look.

'Listen I was only joking, calling it a racket.'

'Yes and I might have been some simpleton who would have believed you, you great big publishing tycoon.'

'You're mad at me. Let me buy you the best dinner that money can buy.'

'That would be one without you.' She was not angry, just bored. The result was to make him angry.

'All right then. I haven't met many aristocrats over here and those I've met have been a seedy second-rate lot,' he snapped back at her. 'I thought you would be different. Seems I was wrong.'

'We're people like anyone else. What did you expect? Haloes shaped like coronets? Why not go and peddle your books somewhere else Mr. Manisty?'

At that moment someone came up behind him.

'Hullo Caroline. Sorry I'm a few minutes late.'

'Hullo Richard. Just in time. Let's go and have a nice cool drink.'

Magnus turned and glared. The man standing just behind him was a trifle shorter than himself, dark-haired with a trim dark moustache. He had a lean, distinguished look, and was young and slender. He was beautifully dressed in a dark suit.

'Sorry old boy,' Richard Verney said pleasantly. 'Did I interrupt you?'

'No old boy,' was the sarcastic reply. 'I'm just leaving. Are you one of the guides?'

Magnus strode off towards the side door and Richard Verney raised his eyebrows as his eyes followed the departing American.

'Disgruntled customer darling?' he asked Caroline.

'You could call him that. Guess who he is.'

'A basketball player perhaps? Should I know him?'

'No, he works for Laker & Day, the publishers. That book on stately homes is one of the things he looks after.'

'Really? How odd. I'd have thought that was an Englishman's job. What's he doing here? Looking for material?'

'No, just another customer, come to see what it's like.'

'I hope I wasn't rude. I thought he was some tourist asking questions.'

'He *is* a visitor, he *was* asking a question, and you weren't at all rude! There's Aunt Selina. I'm free for twenty minutes. Come into the sitting-room and have a lemonade.'

Richard Verney tucked her arm through his and they went out through the side door. Just outside Lord Vivian Eaton, the 7th Earl of Thornbury, sat flexing his right hand. He had been signing brochures since ten in the morning. He believed in showing himself to the public — they rather liked to have a real peer on

24

display. He also believed that signing the brochures was one of the things that kept the visitors coming. He wore a Donegal tweed sports coat with cavalry cord slacks, and looked what he was — one of a long line of English country gentlemen. When he saw Caroline and Richard he smiled.

'Hullo you two. It's been a busy day. How are things with you Caroline?'

'I've been slacking, and now I'm going to have a lemonade with Richard before I take the next party round. Oh, and I met someone.'

She told him quickly about Magnus Manisty.

'Where's he gone?' her father asked, showing unexpected interest.

'I don't know,' Caroline replied. 'Somewhere out there. Why?'

'I'd like to talk to him.'

'If I see him I'll tell him,' she promised without visible enthusiasm.

'I wish you would. I ought to stick at this till four o'clock at least.'

'What do you want to see him for?' Caroline asked.

'Business,' her father replied vaguely. 'Things I want to discuss. I was going to write to Laker & Day soon anyway. Jolly good luck his showing up like this.'

Caroline made a face at Richard who suppressed a laugh. They left the earl to his pile of brochures and his trusty gold ballpen. At the rear of the house was a wing over which visitors were not shown. Here the family lived. It had four bedrooms, a sitting-room, dining-room, a library, and a lovely private walled garden. This was their private retreat. It was also, in winter, the only really warm part of the house.

'You know,' Richard Verney said thoughtfully while Caroline poured lemonade from a jug in which ice cubes tinkled invitingly. 'I'd rather like to talk to that American myself, come to think of it.'

'What is it he has?' Caroline asked tartly. 'Sex appeal or something?'

Richard grinned. 'No, but I do want

26

some advice. He might be able to help.'

'If you're still wondering how to do something with Verney Hall, then Magnus Manisty is the last person to ask. He doesn't know a thing about it. He wanted to take me out so that *I* could give *him* chapter and verse. I refused of course.'

'Of course.' Richard was disappointed.

'I'm your girl.'

He brightened at this reminder. There was no official understanding between them, but neither he nor Caroline had anyone else, and soon, when he was doing better in his uncle's merchant bank in the city, he would get round to discussing the engagement. The engagement was as inevitable as an increase in the cost of living. It was so inevitable in fact that nobody bothered to mention it. It was unnecessary.

2

Magnus stood in the drive and looked at the people in the tea garden and the others walking to and from the topiary garden. The world had gone dull. The trees and grass were no longer green, they were a drab, soupy grey. People were no longer happy and smiling. They had become Hogarthian and horrid. The sun had disappeared. There was *vivre* but no *joie*. The cause was not difficult to discern. Lady Caroline Eaton knocked every other girl he had ever seen into a cocked hat — and Lady Caroline Eaton was high-hatting him quite unmistakably. Worse still, they were poles apart. She was upper crust English and quite probably thought of the Conqueror as *nouveau riche*. She had nothing in common with a Yank whose grandfather had jumped ship in Boston and was an illegal resident in the U.S.A. all his life, although nobody ever discovered the fact. His grandfather had been a carpenter and his father had owned a small grocery store. He, the bright young man of publishing, still all prospects with very little solid achievement, was the nearest thing to a success story the family had. What had he in common with seventh earls and stately homes, open to the public or otherwise?

It was so completely unlike him to feel self-conscious that he considered taking to strong drink. Something however impelled him back towards the house. He decided to buy a brochure and get the pleasant looking man sitting at the side door to autograph it for him. He turned and retraced his steps.

Vivian Eaton looked up and smiled.

'Can I have one of the booklets, autographed please? Or better still, make it two,' Magnus said, producing a pound note.

'With pleasure.' Vivian took two booklets off the top of the pile and wondered at the accent. Could this be the man Caroline mentioned?

'You're the earl?' Magnus asked.

'Guilty. You aren't by any chance the chappie from Laker & Day, are you?'

'How did you know?' Magnus showed astonishment.

'My daughter mentioned you. You're just the chap I wanted to see.'

Absentmindedly he pocketed the pound.

'What about?' Magnus asked.

'I can't really say much here. Too liable to interruption. Can you stay till four?'

'Yes.'

'Then meet me here at four and we'll adjourn to my den for something to drink and a chat. I could do with some advice.'

Magnus brightened. If he could not get in by kicking down the front door, why not sneak in the back way? Besides he liked the look of the seventh earl. He seemed a thoroughly decent guy.

Miraculously the sun blazed forth,

flowers suddenly blossomed, fat ladies with halitosis looked like Gainsborough portraits, and their stringy husbands seemed like members of a master race. Even noisy, disobedient children took on the aspect of little angels. Magnus bought a ticket from the vendor at the entrance to the maze, and almost lost himself as a result. He kept his appointment by the skin of his teeth and by following a family whose offspring had been beset by an overwhelming desire to visit one of the places delicately labelled 'Convenience'.

'Ah there you are.' Vivian Eaton beamed. 'What a day. I've got writer's cramp. Four hundred and ten I make it. That's not far from the record. So early in the year too. Come along and see where the poor owners live.'

He led the way to the private part of the house and soon they were sitting relaxed in the library.

'What do you drink? I've got whisky, brandy, some beer I think . . . '

'I'm a non-drinker.'

'Are you? Good, so am I. I've got some barley water, or there's tomato juice I believe. I expect you like tomato juice.'

'I do.'

'Or tea?'

'Tomato juice, please.'

Vivian rang a bell and the maid appeared. He asked her to bring a jug of tomato juice with ice cubes in it and she went off. Magnus approved of him even more.

'No port and cigars?' he asked mildly. 'I thought it went with the job.'

'Lots of people do, dear boy. Lots of people do. I hate both. Now, tell me about your work.'

'Not much to tell,' Magnus replied, and gave his host the salient details.

Vivian nodded. 'Splendid. Listen, I want to get a proper book written. History of the house and the family, you know? Other places do it. You can sell a decent hard cover book for £1, you know.'

'You'd be pushed to print it for as

little as that,' Magnus warned.

'I thought we could sell it at almost cost price and then once we'd sold so many, it would be all profit.'

'I see. How many would you reckon to sell in a year?'

'We get thirty thousand visitors. Say perhaps a quarter of that. Seven thousand? I think that could be done. Better be safe and say five thousand.'

'That's different. Could you really sell five thousand copies a year?'

'If I could sell it for 99p, I could,' the astute earl stated firmly.

'Then if you were prepared to wait a year for profit it might be done.'

'Good lord yes. Wait two years if necessary. It would come off taxes as a business expense, anyway. I thought if the printing job cost maybe five thousand plus another five or six hundred for someone to write it, it would be viable. But I wanted to talk to you.'

'Do you have material for the book?'

'Lord yes, this room is full of books

about us, old ones. I want something up-to-date and snappy. Lots of scandal about Charles II and my ancestress alone in that octagon room playing whatever they played, eh?'

'I see. Well, I suppose I could help.'

'Ah, that's what I hoped. The first problem of course is to find a writer.'

'I could write it for you,' Magnus said confidently.

'You could? I didn't know you were a writer.'

'Honours degree in English Literature.'

'Sorry. I had no idea.'

'It wouldn't cost you anything either.'

'I should insist,' Vivian contradicted.

'No, no. One doesn't ask for money. Of course I would like to spend a lot of time here, researching. Perhaps I could come to stay at weekends?'

'Stay permanently old chap.'

'There's my job to consider. I'd have to come over on Saturdays and Sundays.'

'Of course. Make yourself at home.'

'I know a quality printer who would give us a good price. Until I know more about the length and the illustrations I can't be too precise, but I don't think you'll need your five thousand pounds.'

'If we printed ten thousand copies . . .'

'No need to print so many. We'll print enough to cover the cost and we'll leave the type standing so that a reprint will be comparatively cheap. You'll make all your profits on the reprints. Do a year's supply at a time and write off the initial costs in the first year and make a profit on all subsequent years.'

'By jove that's good business,' Vivian said delightedly. 'A nice tax loss in the first year and profits thereafter. Can it be done?'

'I don't see why not. We'll have to spend some time working out the print order and the costs, but I don't see why not. You want to sell at 99p?'

'Definitely. I can sell twenty per cent more at 99p than I can at £1.'

'You should be in publishing.'

'Really? Kind of you to be so flattering, but I've no head for business. I know a little bit about this place after ten years of charging people to get inside, but that's all I know.'

'How does it work?' Magnus asked looking innocent, and the reply, which lasted for forty minutes, delighted him. At the end of it he felt that he knew more about the stately home business than any other commoner in the country.

'We've been talking all about Portcullis,' Vivian said suddenly. 'Look here, where do you live?'

'Richmond.'

'Got a car?'

'Yes.'

'That's fine. You must stay to dinner. We usually have it at eight-thirty on a Saturday, after everybody has gone. It's only a salad tonight, do you mind?'

'Not at all. I like it.'

'Good. Now tell me about yourself. Where do you come from?'

'Putney.'

'I thought you were American. Putney's next door to Richmond.'

'No. Putney in Vermont.'

'My God, you've got a Putney over there too? Who'd have believed it.'

'It *is* called New England, sir.'

'Don't call me sir, please. Vivian is the name. The family call me Viv. In Vermont, you say?'

'Between Brattleboro and Bellows Falls.'

'Fascinating names. What do you do there?'

'After college I went to New York for a couple of years in publishing, and then I got the chance to come over here with Laker & Day. That was three years ago.'

'Do you plan to stay here?'

'I may do. It depends on how things go.'

'How did you get a job with a British publisher?'

'We own them.'

'Who is we?' Vivian asked.

'Hammarton Publishing in New York.

We have several companies over here.'

'So you are really still with the same firm, is that it?'

'Yes, I guess so. If I make the grade they will probably keep me in Britain for a long time. I think I'd like that.'

'Do you ever go back to America at all?'

'On vacation, to see my parents.'

'It sounds a pleasant life. You must be good at your job.'

'Not bad,' Magnus agreed. 'I get by at it. I should be what they call editorial director of Laker & Day in a couple of years and then, if I play my cards right, a transfer to a bigger company in the group, as a director, and finally chairman one day. I might even get to the board of Hammarton Holdings one day. That's real success.'

'Does it pay?' Vivian asked bluntly. Money interested him. He had so nearly gone broke that he had never quite recovered from it and was always on the look out for financial information.

'Quite well. I've got a nice flat and a

Porsche, and I save.'

'In these days that's a miracle.'

'You're not doing too badly are you?'

'Thanks mainly to my solicitor, Bertram Batty. He's the brains behind this. I'd have ended up on social security if it hadn't been for him. It isn't myself I worry about, it's Caroline. You met her yourself. She's a lovely girl. I don't want to see her spend the rest of her life slaving over a kitchen sink.'

'Is there any danger of that?'

'No. Young Verney wants to marry her. You haven't met him I suppose. He's a pleasant fellow. He lives with his mother at a ghastly Victorian place called Verney Hall near Weybridge, about three miles away. His father was a proper bad hat. He recently died in America, incidentally, after enthusiastically pursuing wine, women and gambling saloons. I think he passed away in Las Vegas. Strange fellow. Anyway Richard works in his uncle's bank.'

'Nice to have an uncle with a bank,'

Magnus commented dryly.

'Very,' Vivian agreed with a quick nod. 'Lord Binfield is his name and he owns part of Verney's Bank in the City. Richard is something in the office.'

'Charming.' The sarcasm was not well concealed and Vivian glanced up.

'Have you met him?'

'Is he the one who looks rather like David Niven? Dark moustache and crinkly hair?'

'That's right. About your own age.'

'I met him briefly.'

'He's full of charm. He and Caroline will marry one day. Of course Richard has no money of his own, but if he's a banker he should be able to help Caroline to run this place profitably.'

'No money when they own a bank?'

'Old Binfield is meaner than Scrooge, believe me, and anyway he's only a part owner nowadays. He pays Richard a beggarly salary, but he does teach him things.'

'What do they live on?'

'Richard's mother has a little bit, not

much. In fact they're trying to do something with Verney Hall, but it has no natural attractions. We've got that wonderful octagon room which baffles everybody, and the lovely gardens. It gave us something to work with. Bertram says you can't do a thing with Verney Hall, and he ought to know.'

'I see. I'd have thought your daughter might do better for herself than marry a bank clerk.'

'They'll be all right. He can sell that awful house when his mother dies and sink the capital in this place. It's a good investment. I want to develop it.'

'It looks pretty good as it is,' Magnus remarked.

'Ah, that's just where you're wrong. This is like any other business. You can't stand still. The competition is ferocious, and some of them light their cigars with thousand pound cheques. I've got to struggle to survive.'

'What you want is a museum, an interesting one.'

'What sort of interesting one?' Vivian

asked, perking up at this suggestion. 'We can't do vintage cars, it's already been done and anyway, they're far too expensive nowadays.'

'Clocks perhaps.'

'Clocks?'

'I once visited a place in Illinois called Rockford. It's got a Time Museum. That's an idea. You should be able to pick up old clocks and watches. What you want is an agent, someone in the business.'

'It's an idea. I'd thought of armour but again it's so damned expensive, and everybody else is collecting it. Nobody is interested in what I collect.'

'Do you collect?'

'Lord yes, ever since I was a boy. I'm a deltiologist among other things.'

'What's that?'

'I collect postcards. My father started it. He was a bit weak in the head really, poor old chap. Charming but stupid. Honesty forces me to admit it. He collected postcards and I've kept it up. I've got thousands. Some good ones too. Worth a few hundred pounds.'

'That's great.'

'And I do tea cosies and muffs.'

'Muffs?'

'What women used to shove their hands into to keep warm. I've got about a hundred. I've got a good selection of old tea cosies too.'

'What do you do with them?'

'There's an attic room where I keep what I call 'The Collection'.'

'Look here sir, you must put these on show and charge 20p to get in.'

'I only charge ten for the maze.'

'Make it twenty next year. Get a little room or a garden hut or something. Show your collection. And I'd have a go at the time museum. I don't think anyone else is doing that. Do you know Insoles in London?'

'The clockmakers? I've heard of them. I think we have a couple of really old Insoles clocks in the house.'

'I'll go to see them and see about a collection. If I sweet-talk them a bit, they might help for a small commission.'

'I could charge that up to tax, couldn't I?'

'I expect so. I'll talk to our tax accountant.'

'Will you really?' Vivian asked.

'Leave it to me.'

'I can't think why you are so kind. After all, we're practically strangers.'

'Ah,' Magnus answered with a wink, 'but not for long. I'm doing the history of the Eatons of Portcullis, aren't I?'

'So you are. That practically makes you one of the family.'

'I can't think of anything I'd like better,' Magnus said, thinking of Caroline. 'I honestly can't.'

Vivian thought that he was quite an unusually nice person.

★ ★ ★

'What are you doing here?' Caroline hissed.

Magnus winked.

'Don't wink at me. Answer me, you . . . you . . . oh, I can't think of a word.'

'Call me one of the family. You heard your father. I'm writing the book of the film.'

'Very funny. How did you worm yourself into my father's friendship like that, you snake?'

'Watch it. He wouldn't like that sort of talk. We met, he wanted to discuss business, we discussed business, and here I am. Staying to dinner. I'll be over next Saturday morning to spend the weekend working here in the library.'

'Will you indeed!'

'Nothing can stop it. I did it all for you.'

'What does that mean?' she asked suspiciously. Her father was out of the room, and Richard had gone home. She and Magnus had the study to themselves.

'I fell for you the moment I clapped eyes on you. Don't you like that? There's a prime piece of old English. Clapping eyes. I adore the sound of it. It's so much more expressive than saying 'noticed you' or 'saw you' or something wishy-washy. I clapped eyes on you, Lady Caroline Eaton, and the applause is deafening.'

'Is that meant to be a joke again? Like galley slave?'

'My priceless prose is wasted on you.'

'You aren't a writer.'

'True, but I come into contact with them. I thought it was brushing off quite nicely.'

'Then what's this about you writing our history?'

'You don't want James Michener for a job like that. Why pay someone when you can have it done for nothing? I'll write it, and having done that, I'll edit it. Editing it is something I *can* do. I do it all the time. What's more, I've got staff who help me. This is what you English call a piece of cake.'

'What's in it for you?' she demanded.

'Nothing.' He looked hurt. 'Not a darned thing. Just hard work and spending all my free time here.'

'Spending all your free time here?'

'Research,' he explained. 'That's important.'

'You could take books home with you.'

'Much better to do it on the spot. Your father agreed. I like him, incidentally. I didn't know earls could be so human. He's just like a real person.'

'Oh very funny.'

'I thought you'd appreciate it. Where did junior go?'

'Junior?' She scowled as his meaning became clear to her. 'You mean Richard? He had to go home.'

'To mother?'

'I'd be glad if you would stop being nasty about my friends. You are a guest in this house after all.'

'An honoured one, cross my heart. I'm going to see your father's postcards after dinner. We have plans for those postcards. They are going to earn a lot of money for your old age, believe me.'

'They are?' She forgot to snap at him. 'Why?'

He explained some of what was in his

mind and she listened, forgetful of his earlier banter.

'What made you think of all this?' she asked.

Instead of a quick quip he got up and walked to the window, with its small diamond shaped panes, and looked out at the garden beyond. He turned and his face was in the shadow.

'I'm not sure. I suppose that like anyone else on the outside, I'm intensely curious about a place like this. You probably don't realise it, but there is a mystique about earls that is quite overpowering, and the mass of us have no idea what it feels like to own a queer eight-sided room, with no windows, where Charles II once misbehaved himself with someone else's wife.

'Life can be a very drag, mundane affair. Not yours, perhaps, but mine and others. So my interest is perfectly ordinary and natural. For the rest, well I like problems. I like solving them. When your father talked about developing the place, I thought of what might interest people. I suppose in a way that what I'm doing is playing make believe. If this house were mine, what would *I* do with it? There's nothing sinister about me. Honestly.'

'I'm sorry. You're so flip sometimes that I don't know when to take you seriously.'

'That's my armour against life. You aren't meant to know.'

'You're doing all this for nothing?'

'For the love of it. Also because of you.'

She flushed at that. 'I'm not sure I understand you, and I'm not sure I want to.'

'Love at first sight,' he said quite seriously.

'I don't believe you.'

'It can happen. I wouldn't have believed it myself till today. It wasn't that way with Lisette . . . '

'Who's Lisette?' she asked flatly.

'That was a slip. She's a girl and we had a fight. She was meant to come here with me today, but I'm glad now she didn't.'

'You're on the rebound? I don't call that love at first sight. Anyway I don't believe in it.'

'It's nothing to do with being on the rebound,' he answered hotly. 'Besides there is only one sort of love that matters, the sort that turns you upside down and stands you on your head, the sort that makes a complete nonsense of life. I've never experienced it before today.'

'I don't think this sort of talk is funny.'

'My God, it's not meant to be funny,' he said heatedly. 'Do you think I'm chatting you up? I want to marry you.'

'You don't waste time.'

'I haven't got any time to waste. I expect to live to 110 and nearly twenty-seven years of that have gone already, frittered away without so much as a sight of you. I've only got eighty-three years left. I'm working on life extension, but at the moment 110 is the best I can manage if I want to stay fit at the same time.'

'You're a lunatic.'

'That's part of my inimitable charm,' he agreed. 'I'll give you a day or two to get used to it. Meantime you'd better tell your friend Richard Verney to work hard at banking and leave the stately home business to others.'

'I've known Richard all my life. I shall marry him.'

'Are you engaged?'

'Not officially,' she hedged.

'I thought not. You'll never marry him. A girl like you can't marry a bank clerk.'

'What are you?' she asked sweetly. 'An office boy?'

'I'm about to revolutionise the stately home business. This place is only seventeen miles from London, it is on the Thames, it is a natural. I intend to turn it upside down before I'm finished. You'll have the Queen of England coming to buy a ticket to see it. You wait.'

'Did someone mention the Queen?' a voice asked and they turned to see

Vivian who had just come into the room.

'I said that before I'm finished, she'll be queueing up to visit Portcullis,' Magnus told him.

'Nothing would surprise me. What do you have in mind?'

'I'd rather not say now. Wait till next weekend. You're going to get a lot more out of me than a history of the house and family.'

'Grand. I can hardly wait. Would you like to see my muffs before dinner?'

'I'd love that.'

'Coming, Caroline?'

'No thanks Daddy. You two go by yourselves. I'll stay here till dinner time.'

They went out, Magnus turning and winking at her. She stared after him, disturbed. She had never really known an American before, and she was unsure of him. He represented an unknown quantity. What's more, he was a disturbing sort of unknown quantity. She had a funny feeling that he might be able to accomplish some of his boasts. She turned and looked out of the windows and crossed her arms over her chest. She shivered momentarily. She was an inveterate reader of horoscopes. That morning hers had warned '*The time has come to deal firmly with a 'snake' in your paradise! Weekends are fun.*'

The weekend might be fun, but who was the snake she wondered? Magnus didn't look at all like a snake.

Why should he be so interested in them? She knew she was pretty and had always been pleased by the fact. Why not? It made life more pleasant and interesting. However, she had never had such a dramatic effect on a man before. Suppose he thought they were rich? Or suppose he thought that if he married her he'd get a title, which he wouldn't.

Suppose he really had fallen in love at first sight . . .

Suddenly she was glad that he had come into their lives.

3

It was late but Magnus showed no signs of wishing to go home. Vivian, who was not slow on the uptake, decided that he was playing gooseberry in his own home, finished his coffee and left Caroline and Magnus together. 'I suppose I ought to go,' Magnus said unconvincingly.

'It has been rather a hectic day and tomorrow will be another,' Caroline agreed. 'I'm tired.'

'I'm not. It must be the company. You know, I'm glad I stopped and talked to your father. I like him and I'm interested in what you are doing here.'

'So you said before.'

'Did I? Well, it's worth repeating. I shall be coming back tomorrow, of course.'

'You *will*?' Caroline blinked at him.

'Naturally. Might as well get to work

quickly. While your father practises his signature and you explain to people the finer points of the very elegant furniture in the octagon room, I shall be right in the library poring over books and making notes.'

'I don't think Daddy knows you're coming tomorrow.'

'I didn't mention it. I took it for granted. He wants me to start in on writing a book, so start I shall.'

'I see.'

'Don't worry, no more nasty cracks. I'm on the team now.'

'Thank you.' She spoke ironically.

'Do you ever come to Richmond?' he asked hopefully.

'Hardly ever. Occasionally I drive through it.'

'Pity. Of course after Portcullis nothing is likely to impress you, but Richmond has its points.'

'What was Daddy trying to say about Putney? I didn't follow.'

'Nothing special. I was born in Putney . . . Putney, Vermont.'

'How odd.'

'I bet you haven't heard of it?'

'I haven't,' she agreed.

'Or Manchester, Dorset, Rutland, Londonderry, Dover or Ludlow — all in Vermont.'

She shook her head dumbly and he laughed.

'There's a bigger Manchester next door in New Hampshire. We're called New England, remember.'

'What sort of place is Putney?'

'Not very big. We have Santa's Land.'

'What's that?' She leaned forwards.

'The home of Santa Claus. It's quite a thing. There's a Christmas Tree Shop, a Candy Cane Cupboard and a Santa's Alpine Railroad. You ought to come and see it some time.'

'It's rather far to go just to see Santa Claus, don't you think?'

'Depends on the sort of person you are, doesn't it?' he countered. 'Some people would cross the world to see what's at the end of the rainbow; others just sit at home and say there's nothing.'

'What does that mean?'

'What it says. There are two kinds of people. Do you believe in fairies?'

'That's a ridiculous sort of question.'

'I hope you don't mean that. If you don't believe in fairies we can't be friends.'

'I thought you were a hard hearted publisher.'

'Why hard hearted? Sure, I know it's a hard world and you can't sell a book by giving it a pretty cover — you need a sales drive. That doesn't make *me* hard hearted.'

'I suppose you believe in Santa Claus?' she asked disparagingly.

'Got to. I come from Santa Land, U.S.A.'

'Before you go,' she said, thereby reminding him that he was not staying for the night, 'where on earth did you get that tan at this time of the year?'

'The Seychelles. I was there two weeks ago, on a short holiday.'

'Why the Seychelles?' she asked, surprised.

'To try the water ski-ing. I heard of an American who runs a water ski operation. It's good. Worth the visit.'

'You ski?'

'Snow and water. I was brought up on snow skis. Lots of ski-ing in Vermont. I took to water ski-ing in the summer.'

'Nice if you can afford it.'

'You're not all that poor, Caroline.'

'No. I didn't mean that. It's just that in this country practically nobody can say that they were brought up on skis. I'm envious.'

'You needn't be. What do you do with your spare time?'

'I used to play tennis but I'm a bit out of practice nowadays. There always seems to be plenty to do around the house. My mother's dead.'

'Of course. Sorry. Don't you go away for holidays?'

'I went to Wales pony trekking last year, and the year before I went for a sailing holiday.'

'You need organising.'

'I do not,' she said very definitely. 'I don't like anyone organising me.'

'I keep saying the wrong things don't I?' he laughed. 'I must let you get some rest. See you in the morning. Oh, what time do you get up?'

'Eight. Why?'

'I don't want to arrive too early. I'll be here at eight-thirty.'

'You needn't come that early,' she exclaimed.

'I want to. I am drawn as though by a magnet.' He stood up and winked. 'I hope your friend Richard will be at Church or something.'

'Richard will probably be here. He usually comes to see me on a Sunday.'

'You shouldn't encourage him,' Magnus said quite seriously. 'The poor fellow might get all the wrong ideas.'

'It's time you went,' Caroline said abruptly and stood up.

'I believe you want me to go.' He laughed. 'It's been a day of surprises for me.'

'I'm sure your girlfriend will be

interested to hear all about it.'

'My what?'

'You did mention a girl.'

'That was nothing serious. She's a nice girl but I don't expect I'll be seeing her again. She has a career to worry about.'

'You don't sound very concerned.'

'There isn't any cause for concern. You needn't look so disapproving. Her last words to me were 'Drop dead'.'

He laughed as he spoke, and Caroline could not help smiling. She showed him to the door and was relieved when he did not try to kiss her. He looked the type who might very easily chance it. A moment or two later she heard the sound of his car engine from the car park at the side of the house, and then the roar of the exhaust fading as he headed for the main road. With a little sigh she shut up house and went to bed.

She was surprised when the telephone rang just as she was about to get into bed, and with an impatient gesture she put on her dressing-gown and walked along the corridor to the extension at the top of the stairs.

'Portcullis Manor,' she announced frigidly.

'Caroline?'

'Richard! What do you want at this time of night?'

'I wanted to ask you something.'

Caroline could not have been more surprised if the Prime Minister had telephoned to ask her to tea at No. 10. Richard simply didn't telephone people late at night. Richard led a regulated, orderly life.

'What is it?' she demanded, intrigued.

'Will you marry me?'

Caroline took a deep breath.

'If this is a joke, Richard, I am not amused.'

'It isn't a joke. I mean it. I suddenly felt that it was time we decided. I won't be able to sleep a wink until you agree.'

'What's got into you?'

The oddity of the situation struck her forcibly.

'I don't know,' he answered; but deep down he knew very well.

He had seen her talking to the American, and for the first time his confidence was shaken. There was something so capable, so self-sufficient, so confident about Magnus that Richard's own self-sufficiency had been dented. His Old-Etonian composure had begun to crumble. Magnus Manisty looked like the sort of man who could do anything and do it well. Suppose Caroline fell for that All-American-Boy charm of his? It was possible, although Caroline had indicated that she was unimpressed. Richard knew better than to take anything a woman said at its face value. His mother had warned him about that; and strangely enough it had never occurred to him that his mother was a woman too and that perhaps he shouldn't take what *she* was saying at its face value. All he knew was that for once he was uneasy about Caroline. All had been set fair, but now there was a small dark cloud on the far horizon, and he decided to act.

'Do you really want an answer at eleven-thirty at night?' she demanded.

'Are you angry?' he asked.

'No. You are an idiot Richard, telephoning like this.'

'Are we engaged?' he demanded to know.

'Yes, I suppose so.'

'Properly engaged — ready to buy a ring and pop a notice in *The Times* for all to read?'

'If that's what you want.'

'Thank God for that.'

'You sound relieved. Did you think I was going to run away with old Mr. Cook or someone?'

'No. I suppose I just woke up to the fact that nothing has ever been settled. It's settled now, isn't it? Definitely?'

'Yes Richard.'

'Then I'll see you tomorrow. Thanks Caroline.'

As she hung up she frowned. '*Thanks* Caroline'? It was an odd thing to say under the circumstances. Not once had he called her 'dear' or 'darling'. Well, she thought as she reached her bedroom and took off her dressing-gown, it was settled now. It was a sensible arrangement. Her father would approve and so would Mrs. Verney, who so rarely approved of anything. She was doing the right thing.

As she lay in bed it occurred to her that she was trying to convince herself of what she already knew was right. Why was that? It had all been inevitable since that night during her last year at Westonbirt, when they had that rather super dance at Tum-Tum Hutchinson's house and Richard had made his feelings so obvious to everyone that she had been the victim of non-stop badinage all during the last term.

Strangely enough, now that it was out in the open and properly settled, she could not sleep. She put out the light and lay restlessly, her mind unusually active. Richard was slim, dark, beauti-fully mannered, so obviously a model suitor who would turn into a model husband. He was really quite clever and he would be no end of help at Portcullis Manor over the financial side of things. Eton, Oxford, Verney's Bank, Verney Hall — his credentials were gilt edged, and he was even good looking in a sort of Byronic way (thank God he didn't have any other Byronic characteristics!).

It was quite late before sleep came and it brought a vivid dream in which Richard was standing at the gates of Portcullis taking money, but he would not let her in. She was quite glad when she woke up early, feeling irritable, and discovered that it had only been a stupid dream.

★ ★ ★

Aunt Selina, who was twelve years older than her brother and was thus sixty-eight, was always first up in the mornings. She was a dedicated spinster who led a surprisingly full and satisfying existence, and belonged to dozens of societies, clubs and associations in

London. Her mail was staggeringly large and she wrote about half a dozen letters a day every day of her life. Nobody had the faintest idea what they were about. When Caroline went down to breakfast Aunt Selina was already drinking coffee and munching toast with her favourite ginger marmalade.

'Ha, good morning my dear. You look tired.'

'I didn't sleep well.'

'I've told you before, half a pint of hot milk, with some Robertland's Raspberry Yeast Extract in it before going to bed is better than anything else. It's positively good for your health and you'll sleep like a baby. Of course you can get it plain, but the raspberry is much nicer. There's pineapple now too,' she added helping herself to more wholemeal toast.

'Yes aunt.'

'I heard the telephone. Who was it? Another wretched wrong number late at night?'

'No, it was Richard.'

'At *that* time of night?' Aunt Selina looked up amazed. 'I thought his mother put him to bed at ten.'

'That isn't funny.'

'Perhaps it is half past ten.'

Caroline did not reply. She helped herself to coffee to which she added two Sweetex.

'Well, what did he want?' Aunt Selina asked impatiently.

'He asked me to marry him.'

'Good heavens. You mean he telephoned just to ask that — and nearly at midnight too?'

'Yes.'

'Was he sober?'

'Richard doesn't drink.'

'Well, what got into him? He comes here every Sunday, rain or shine, like a puppy on its daily outing.'

'I wish you'd stop making snide remarks about my fiance,' Caroline complained.

'You *agreed*? You're engaged?'

'What did you expect?' Caroline demanded, staring. 'Everyone has always known.'

'That didn't mean it would come off. I thought you had more sense. He's quite unsuitable.'

'What a strange thing to say. You've never said it before.'

'I thought it was unnecessary. You seemed so sensible.'

'How is he unsuitable?'

'He's not your type. He's too phlegmatic, too colourless. I hear he was at Eton for two years before they realised he'd arrived and sent his father a bill for fees.'

'That's unfair and untrue.'

'Sorry. You'd better break it off, though.'

'I shall do no such thing. He's just the sort of husband I want. I shan't have to worry what he's up to, not like some men. He's kind, polite, attentive . . . oh, I could go on for hours.'

'He's like milk — full of goodness, guaranteed harmless and totally unin-spiring.'

'Really.'

'I'm sorry my dear, but I thought you

were keeping him around as a sort of house pet until a real man turned up. Someone like that American who came to dinner last night.'

'That American has a girl of his own with whom he has quarrelled, and anyway he's a complete stranger. He's far too cocky for his own good. He's bumptious.'

'My goodness, you did find out a lot about him in one day, didn't you? Well, I only meant someone like him — someone positive and alive.'

'Who's positive and alive?' Vivian asked coming into the room.

'That American boy. Manisty wasn't it? Guess what Vivian. Caroline has gone and got engaged to Richard Verney.'

'When?' Vivian asked, turning to his daughter.

The business of the telephone call was explained again. He kissed her affectionately.

'I'm so glad Bunny,' he said using an old childhood nickname. 'I hope you're going to be terribly happy.'

'Aunt Selina thinks I made a mistake.'

'Mistake of her life,' Selina agreed unabashed. 'I hope it is going to be a very long engagement so that there will be lots of time to break it off.'

'What on earth do you have against Richard?' Vivian asked his sister as he helped himself to a large breakfast from the hot plate.

'Nothing serious. He'd make a splendid husband for that friend of Caroline's, Augusta Bailey. She's bossy and he needs to be bossed. I should say he's probably a champion doormat. That's not at all what Caroline needs. She needs someone more positive and dynamic.'

'At least he has his hair cut and washes,' Caroline said peevishly.

'Well of course he's clean, but I'd hardly have thought that had much to do with marriage. There must be other men who wash.'

'I think you're unfair,' Vivian remarked

mildly. 'This is Caroline's celebration. She's just got herself engaged. You really mustn't spoil it all by airing your views on suitable husbands.'

'I hope you'll be very happy,' Selina said turning to Caroline, and giving her a charming smile. 'Happy with someone else,' she muttered under her breath, unrepentantly.

'Thank you. I intend to be.'

'When's the wedding to be?' Vivian enquired.

'We haven't talked about that sort of thing, Daddy. Richard will come here about eleven o'clock as usual. We can talk about it later on. I'm not in any hurry. Next year, I expect.'

'I must say he's been faithful to you for years. I don't think he's looked at another girl since he came down from Oxford three or four years ago. You're a lucky girl.'

'Of course I am,' Caroline agreed giving her aunt a look which dared her to open her mouth.

Selina got up.

'I must go and write some letters before the plebeians arrive. I met such a nice little man yesterday. It turned out he works at Sothebys. He was most interesting.'

She paused by the door. 'Is that American boy coming back today?'

'Yes,' Caroline admitted. 'Quite soon too, I expect.'

'Good. I must have a long talk with him.'

She went out and Vivian turned to Caroline.

'Magnus is coming today did you say?'

'So he said last night. He said he wants to get stuck into the job of reading all about the family and the house.'

'Splendid. I liked him.'

'You'd better telephone Laker & Day tomorrow when they open, and check up on him. We don't actually know anything at all about Magnus Manisty except what he has told us. If he's going to have the run of the place we might as well be prudent.'

'I suppose you're right. He could walk off with all the snuff boxes or the family silver, but somehow I don't think he will, do you?'

'No,' Caroline admitted grudgingly, 'but do check.'

'You don't dislike him do you?'

'I think he may be just what you've been looking for. I expect he is extremely clever and gets things done,' she answered. 'His trouble is that he is good and he knows it — at least that's my impression.'

'My trouble always was that I was no good and couldn't disguise it,' Vivian remarked placidly and Caroline kissed his cheek.

'Nonsense, you're a perfect gentleman.'

'What a ghastly thing to have said about me. I mean, it's not much of an accomplishment is it?'

'Very rare darling,' she smiled. 'They will put you in a glass case when you die.'

'You have a macabre imagination. More coffee?'

While they were finishing breakfast Magnus's car was drawing up outside the house. He wore an open necked shirt and carried a college cardigan slung over his shoulder. In one hand was an expensive Liteflite Senior Executive briefcase. He walked into the hall, through the open door, and looked around. Aunt Selina came downstairs at that moment.

'Oh Mr. Manisty, good morning.'

'Good morning yourself. It's going to be a scorcher, according to my radio. I hope you sell lots of ice creams.'

'We don't sell ice cream.'

'You don't? Good heavens, you must.'

'People drop cartons and paper all over the place.'

'It doesn't matter. You should open an ice cream parlour.'

'Is that what you call them in America? Parlours? In my young day the parlour was a front room reserved

74

for special occasions. Every little house had a parlour where the family sat on Sundays.'

'I mean the other kind,' he laughed. 'Where's Lord Thornbury?'

'Still at breakfast. He likes to take his time. Besides he and Caroline are probably talking about her engagement.'

'Her *what*?'

'Her engagement. You met Richard Verney yesterday didn't you?'

'Twice.' He spoke with a noticeable lack of animation.

'Well, they've been friends for years, and he's had eyes for nobody else ever since university. Now they've agreed to marry,' Selina announced.

'How could they? I didn't leave till late, and he went home early, before dinner.'

'He telephoned.'

'Oh.'

'Late at night. Most unlike him. It doesn't matter, the engagement won't last.'

'Won't it?' He perked up a little.

'No, he's the wrong type altogether. She'll realise it. At least I hope she will. It would be awful if they got married. No woman could possibly quarrel with Richard. He's been brought up to believe that gentlemen never quarrel with ladies. It would be like trying to fight a sponge. Hopeless. What a terrible thing that would be. Anyway, I'm sure Caroline will change her mind.'

'It doesn't look like it, if she has agreed to marry him, does it?' Magnus asked.

'What could she say? I'm not worried.'

Magnus looked round sourly. What had he let himself in for, he wondered? Writing a stupid family history while the gorgeous blonde who was the main attraction went off and got engaged to some useless young scion of the nobility who worked in his uncle's bank. He must be getting soft in the head.

'Come along and say good morning

to them,' Selina exclaimed, taking his arm. 'This way.'

She opened the door and they passed inside where Magnus made polite noises. He did not trouble to say anything about the engagement and Caroline quickly finished her coffee and left. Magnus was persuaded to sit down and have a cup with Vivian who did not think the day had properly started until he had tucked away about five coffees.

'Brought your things I see,' Vivian remarked, alluding to the briefcase.

'Some paper and a couple of notebooks. Nothing much, sir.'

'I told you, don't call me sir. Vivian please.'

'It seems all wrong.'

'Do as you're told,' Vivian grinned. 'Now, I'll see you aren't disturbed in the library. We don't have a proper lunch at weekends. The maid will bring you in a tray and if you want anything you must ring for it. Make yourself at home, what? You'll stay to dinner I trust?'

'Isn't it a sort of family occasion? I did hear your daughter is engaged.'

'Lord yes, I'd forgotten already. But you must stay. The more the merrier.'

'Thank you. Incidentally you must do something about ice cream. I understand you don't sell it here?'

'No, too trippery.'

'Well, Vivian, today is going to be a roasting hot one and people will want it. They *are* trippers, after all, aren't they? You sell coloured postcards don't you? Then I really think you ought to sell ice cream too. You needn't sell it in tubs if you're bothered about litter. Sell it in the tea rooms, in dishes. You've got to have it.'

'It's an old and thorny subject. I've got away with not selling it for years. Must I?'

'I think so, I really do. Try it out.'

'I'll have to order the stuff. It will take a week or two to organise it properly.'

'It will be worth it. Meantime why not phone around and try to get hold of an ice cream man to come here in his van?'

'There's one of those all right. He's wild because we won't let him inside. He used to sit outside the gates. He's from Weybridge.'

'Get hold of him. Now I must get down to some work. Got to earn my supper.'

'Don't overdo it.'

'I shan't,' Magnus promised.

He went into the hall just as Richard arrived. The two of them stopped and stared.

'Hullo,' Richard said. 'You back?'

'No, I went away last night and nobody has seen me since.'

Richard smiled politely at what he imagined must be typical American humour.

'Are you going to be doing some work today?'

'Yes. In the library. All day.'

'Poor you, it's going to be beautiful.'

'I had noticed,' Magnus agreed, an edge to his voice.

'Well, I mustn't keep you. I've got things to discuss with Caroline. See you around.'

Magnus stared at him, noting the immaculate blue blazer with its gilt buttons, the cravat painstakingly carelessly tied, the handkerchief in the left cuff — a mannerism he loathed. Stuffed dummy, he thought uncharitably and turned away trailing his briefcase and old cardigan behind him.

He soon forgot Richard Verney however when he began to browse among the books. He picked out a dozen dealing with the Eatons and Portcullis, and put them on a table by the window. He opened the windows to let in fresh air, breathed in the scent of the flowers and grass outside, and opened one of the books. He was soon deeply immersed in it. He was quite surprised when, some considerable time later, he heard a knock on the door.

'Come in,' he yelled.

The door opened and Richard's head poked round it.

'Ah, there you are. I wondered if you had a bit of time to spare.'

'Yes.'

Richard beamed, shut the door, crossed the room and sat down in a chair facing him.

'I'd like some advice,' he began, and Magnus sat back in his chair and gazed at him unsympathetically.

4

Magnus shook his head as he turned away from the window to look at his caller.

'It's not good,' he said bluntly. 'You can't get into the stately home racket without a stately home.'

'I don't think you ought to keep calling it a racket, old man.'

'Habit. I meant no harm.' Magnus did in fact regard most respectable established activities as rackets but he did not seriously consider that people ought to be put in prison on that account for, on his reckoning, it would leave too few people at liberty to manage the affairs of the world.

'The point is,' Magnus went on, 'that your house is not particularly old, not particularly attractive and has no unusual features. You could, I suppose, spend a small fortune having your grounds landscaped but it wouldn't be worth the capital outlay. Forget it.'

'Oh dear.'

'Don't you inherit part of a bank one day?' Magnus asked frankly.

'A title, but not a bank. Uncle Bill *is* the Chairman, and I daresay they more or less have to find me a job, but the control is with some relations of mine called Firkin. It's all rather complicated but Uncle Bill's shares can't pass to me. They go back to the bank. Verney's Bank will no longer be in Verney hands when he dies — he's only got eighteen per cent of it now, anyway.'

'I'll take your word. It sounds enormously complicated. What's this about a title?'

'I'm Uncle Bill's heir by special remainder. I'll be sixth Baron Binfield one day, and a fat lot of good that will do me,' he added despondently. His mother was the grand-daughter of a duke and he did not think much of mere barons.

'Surely you can do something about that?'

'What?' Richard asked, looking up. 'You mean, give it up? It's not worth the bother.'

'No, far from it. Capitalise on the situation. You're going to be a lord, my lad. That's worth something. Can you play the piano?'

'No.'

'Pity. I could do something with a piano-playing lord. I've a friend. Oh well. What do you do?'

'Nothing much.'

Magnus glared at him, thinking what a wet rag of a man he was.

'What's your sport?' he demanded.

'Nothing these days. I watch Wimbledon on telly.'

'My God. All right, do you have a hobby? Do you collect things?'

'I dabble in photography.'

'Ah, now he tells me. Enlarge on this dabbling.'

It turned out that Richard had a Rolleiflex and was quite a keen amateur photographer in black and white. In fact he waxed eloquent on the subject when Magnus asked him if he did any colour photography.

'No, of course not. If you set the camera properly you just point it and click, it's all done for you. That's not photography. There's no light and shade in colour photography. Really satisfying photographs have got to be black and white. That's where the artistry comes in.'

Magnus considered this and decided that he understood. He nodded.

'Do you do your own printing?'

'Printing and enlarging. I've got some quite good equipment.'

'I'd like to see some of your work.'

'Why? You wouldn't understand it.'

'What do you mean?' Magnus asked.

'I don't photograph people on the beach. I look for odd things — curious angles in walls, odd light and shade effects. You wouldn't enjoy my photographs.'

'You'd be surprised. Couldn't you

photograph people?'

'What for? Do you think I'm going to open up a shop in the High Street?'

'No, of course not, but someone who is going to be a lord can make a fortune out of photographing people.'

'I don't believe it.'

'Let me work on it. I'll come up with the gimmick. The point is, can you bring yourself down to earth long enough to snap some hideous woman, and can you make the result flattering?'

'I suppose I could. I've never tried.'

Magnus was examining a nebulous idea from all angles. He liked playing about with ideas.

'Listen, I've got a friend, a fashion model. If I brought her here could you photograph her against the house? Shoot off a couple of films, and blow the negs up into good full plate prints?'

'Yes. Who is she?'

'Don't go too fast. She may not agree, but I'll try to get Lisette to come here next weekend. You be on hand to do me a pile of photographs, and if I can't set you up in business my name isn't Magnus Manisty.'

'I don't want to be a photographer.'

'Do you want to be rich?'

'Of course.'

'Portraits by Verney of London. It sounds good. If you play hard to get, people will queue up waving cheque books.' Magnus knew a little bit about photography and the cost of doing one's own printing and developing. He also knew what a good studio charged for a portrait. There was money in it somewhere, if one went about it properly.

'Why are you so interested in helping me?' Richard asked. His suspicions had suddenly become roused.

'Why not?' Magnus asked blandly. 'I guess I just like solving problems. That's why I'm here today. I'm trying to help Lord Thornbury develop this place. I'm an ideas man, that's all. I'm not much good when it comes to following through. I'd have done well in advertising — you know, 'I'm only here for the Scrubitoff — it tastes just like real axle oil'. Besides maybe you'll take my photographs for me free of charge.'

'Who is this model you mentioned?' Richard insisted.

'Lisette Taylor. She's a blonde, very good looking. You must have seen her. She models women's fashions, and she's on the front page of almost every glossy woman's magazine in the country week after week.'

'You think I should be a fashion photographer?'

'No, too much competition. Listen, there is a big untapped source of middle class people who have far more money than they ever had before. Two cars, holidays abroad, colour TV, they've got it all. Now I reckon these people would buy good portrait photography. They've heard of Karsh of Ottawa and Cecil Beaton, but they wouldn't know how to go about contacting them. They'd be scared to try. They'd expect a brush off. Suppose they could get Verney of London to do them at twenty-five pounds a head? If they knew you were heir to a barony and belonged to the aristocracy, they'd lap it up. Weren't you at Eton?'

'Yes.'

'Splendid. You don't want to photograph other people who went to Eton, but the thousands who *wish* they had, and now have the money too late. Social climbers. The world is full of them. Act the part, look the part, you can't miss. Assuming, that is, you know how to take a photograph. That's why I want you to try your hand with Lisette. She's a professional model. You should be able to turn up something really outstanding, if you're as good as I think you might be. After that it's just a question of figuring out how to reach the public. You'll have to spend a bit on advertising. You're not short of money are you?'

'No,' Richard answered cautiously.

'Good. Sorry I can't help with Verney Hall, but I don't think you really expected me to, did you? Hadn't that solicitor, Batty, already told you it was no use?'

Richard nodded absently, thinking about photography. What would Caroline say about his photographing a glamorous model? He assumed she was glamorous. He had never heard of Lisette Taylor.

'Look, I've got to do some work. I'll telephone Lisette in the morning and fix up about the photographs. Let me have your telephone number and I'll contact you about it.'

'I still can't understand why you're going to all this trouble.'

'It's my kind nature,' Magnus lied without shame.

As Richard left him to his work, Magnus was calculating the effect Lisette Taylor might have on him. Richard had led a rather sheltered life, and hadn't he the reputation of never having looked at another woman? He was ripe for subversion. Lisette had one characteristic which had always grated on him — she was an out and out snob.

She'd cut a marquess dead any day in favour of a duke. She had never had much luck with her snobbery. She'd be glad to pose for the heir to a barony, he was certain. Glad, too, to help him. There was material here to work with. Given a bit of luck he might separate Caroline from this unworthy young lay-about. He had plans for Caroline and himself.

He began to whistle softly. All was fair in love and war and besides, he might actually be helping Richard Verney in his career. It was a smugly satisfying or satisfyingly smug thought.

★   ★   ★

Considering that she had just become engaged to be married, Caroline found life disappointingly normal. Somehow she had expected a roseate glow to accompany such an important event, with perhaps the faint but unmistakable sound of tinkling bells and birds singing. It was not so. True, Richard had kissed her several times. The trouble was that Richard was so thoroughly inhibited by his upbringing that his kissing left a little to be desired. Given time and practice she was sure she could remedy the situation but meantime she had to accept the fact that his performance fell far short of what one saw frequently on television. She consoled herself with the thought that if he was inexpert, it was from lack of practice and *that* in itself was something in these permissive days. Dear, dull dependable Richard. She was a lucky girl. Hand in hand they would wander along life's straight and narrow path into the sunset. Indeed she could almost see the sunset already.

Later in the afternoon, when she was free from the necessity of helping to show people round Portcullis, she wandered into the library. There she found Magnus, feet up on a table, reading an enormous old book, rather dusty and dirty in appearance. He had a smudge on his face and he glanced up at her with a preoccupied look in his eye. The look soon fled. He grinned delightedly and put down the heavy tome.

'Hullo. What a nice surprise. Come to check up on me?'

'I did wonder how you were getting on.'

'Well,' he answered waving her to a seat, 'I've scanned the shelves. Some library of books you have. I've made a pile in that corner — these are books I want to read first. However there's a stack of old volumes in that corner cupboard, tucked away at the back behind some boxes. That's where I found this beauty.'

'What is it?' she asked, interested.

'It rejoices in the avant garde title of *Antiquarian Miscellanea* and was published by Bascomb and Bascomb of Eastcheap in 1811. Written by some worthy clergyman whose name was The Rev. Wilkins Welbeck, M.A., D.D. It's really fascinating. He must have spent his whole life on it.'

'Is it about Portcullis?' she asked, puzzled.

'Now there you have me. It is not. At least so far as I can tell, it isn't. I'm cheating, for I ought to be reading about the Eatons. However this rather caught my eye. Do you think your father would let me borrow it?'

'Don't bother asking him. You have my permission,' she replied lightly.

'I'll look after it and return it. I have a positive hatred for people who don't return books.'

'What have you accomplished today then?' she asked.

'My dear Caroline, my work is not to be measured like a ditch. I am researching. Don't worry. I'll come up with a nice fifty thousand word volume on the Eatons of Portcullis which will sell to all the tourists provided it has a decent dust jacket. There's no lack of material. The job is simply to sort out the best of it and write it up in a racy, modern manner.'

'You hope.'

'Oh, it will be done and probably quite quickly.'

'Which means we won't have to see you very often?' she asked.

'I know you foolishly agreed to marry that young banking tycoon, but need you be so pointed in your remarks?' he asked in a pained voice. 'I shall probably see a lot of your father while you and the wretched Richard canoodle in the potting shed or wherever it is you go to be alone. I only hope you get over him quickly.'

'You're very rude.'

'I don't want him to have you,' Magnus said cheerfully. 'I rely on your good taste and excellent common sense to prevail. Your engagement is like measles, nothing worse.'

'You're incredibly brash. I suppose all Americans are.'

'You must stop talking about all Americans as if we were baked beans or something. Where is the lucky man, incidentally?'

'Richard had to leave.'

'That's good. Shall we go and have tea again?'

'Have you finished for the day?'

'I think so,' he nodded. 'This is in the nature of a preliminary canter, to see what sort of material I have to work with. I shall take a few books home with me of course. While you and Richard are discussing wedding plans of an evening I shall be in my lonely flat, bent over books, investigating your ancestors. Doesn't it make you feel creepy?'

'Why should it?'

'Suppose Sir Jasper did time in Newgate for debt? Or Sir Roger was banished from court?'

'I expect they were,' she smiled. 'I can't say I'm much bothered.'

'Well, anyway, think of me toiling over my lowly clerical duties while you pursue your aristocratic pleasures.'

'If you must know, I usually work in the garden in the evenings at this time of the year. It's very soothing.'

'Surely you have lots of gardeners. You must have.'

'Of course we have but we have our own private garden, and I help to look after that.'

'You're a traitor to your class,' he warned sadly, and stood up. 'Come along, let's try the toasted teacakes and the burned bohea.'

'It is not burned. It's good tea.'

'I know. I was being flip. Join me Caroline . . . please?'

'Oh very well.' She laughed. 'I might as well.'

'Not what I'd call an enthusiastic response but it suffices.'

They went out together into the sunshine, where crowds of people were wandering about the grounds of the manor in their bright summer attire. He took her arm and steered her to the tea garden and to the same table they had had yesterday, which had just been vacated. They sat down and the waitress from the town stared at them. Lady Caroline and the same man again. It was certainly something to talk about. Magnus ordered the teas and stretched his legs.

'Busy, isn't it?'

'It generally is.'

'Yes, so your father was telling me. We must make it even busier. Eventually I'm going to have to know all about it — if I'm going to make it the mecca of the stately home set.'

'Are you? I thought you were going to write a book.'

'That's only a beginning. I have many ideas. Your father and I have been talking and I think you and he are overlooking all sorts of interesting potentials.'

'You're taking us over, are you?' she demanded.

'You could say that. I'm going to organise things.'

'I didn't know we wanted it.'

'Probably you don't,' he laughed, 'but it will make me happy.'

'I would have thought a man like you would have been much too busy to bother with us,' Caroline told him bluntly. 'Don't tell me you haven't any friends of your own.'

'Of course I've got friends, but they're mostly business friends. I'm pretty much a stranger here. It takes more than three years to bridge the gap. I used to go to a lot of parties when I lived in Kensington, but not now. I got very tired of them. Now I live rather a restricted life.'

'What about your girlfriend?' she demanded.

'Lisette? She's pretty busy as a rule, and anyway she is no longer my girlfriend. I'm not sure she ever was. Just an ordinary friend.'

'I see.'

Tea came and they were silent for a time. Then he asked her about herself, and she unaccountably began to tell him about her mother, who had died very suddenly eight years earlier, and about her school days.

'I suppose you went to Roedean or Benenden, did you?' he suggested.

'No.'

'Really? Heathfield, then?'

'No, I went to a place in Gloucestershire called Westonbirt. It has an arboretum, you see.'

'You mean trees?'

'Yes, but very special. Daddy heard about it, went to see it, and fell in love with it. You probably don't know it but my father is a bit nutty on the subject of trees. He loves them. Anyway he took one look at the arboretum and decided that Westonbirt was the finest school in England. I don't think he ever asked me what the food was like or if I learned anything.'

'What was the food like and did you learn anything?' Magnus enquired obligingly.

'Like all institutional food, nobody liked it very much. It was all right, I suppose. We thrived on it, anyway. As for learning, well I passed a fair number of examinations. What good it did me I'll never know. The grounds really were lovely, and there was fencing, so I wasn't unhappy.'

'Fencing? Have at you, do you mean?

On guard, et cetera?'

'Yes. It's good exercise.'

'I don't doubt it. Well well, I can't quite see you with a sword in hand.'

'Be warned,' she told him darkly. 'I'm a dangerous woman.'

'So it would seem. I've never met a female Captain Blood before. I ski-ed and swam and played a bit of baseball. I was no good at football. I wasn't interested, you see.'

'Shame.'

'That's what the coach said. I was bigger than most of the other kids my age, too. Ski-ing spoiled me for other things. In summer I liked wandering in the woods. I never had very much to do with other kids. I lacked the gregarious bit.'

'Funny, you don't strike me that way,' she told him.

'I've probably changed. People do, you know. Now there's you.'

'What do you mean, 'now there's me'?' she asked, puzzled at this cryptic comment.

'I haven't told you yet, but we're getting married. Once you ditch Richard, that is, and I've ingratiated myself with your noble father.'

'I've no intention of ditching Richard and I'd be glad if you wouldn't talk about my fiance,' she said stiffly.

'Oh dear, you are on your dignity aren't you? Listen Caroline, let me explain.'

He leant across the table, his fair head drawing closer to her golden one. 'I was standing over there — I can see the exact spot from here — and I saw you like a vision. You know, it was as if all my life I'd been waiting. Wheels whirled, alarm bells began to ring, my head swam, my eyes popped out and in, my heart stopped beating. I didn't need it — the blood was racing round all by itself. I felt like Mohammed in the desert the day he invented Islam — you know, I saw a vision. All at once I knew I was going to marry you.'

'Speak for yourself.' She didn't know

how to answer him. He was definitely crazy.

'I am,' he assured her solemnly. 'That's what I'm doing. Look, I'm not doing badly. I get six thousand now and I've got prospects. We won't starve. If you want to stay on here, I shan't mind.'

'Thank you very much, but I do have plans of my own.'

'You can't have,' he protested. 'I told you, I was smitten. Hip and thigh, as the good book says. You don't think Cupid belts into a man like that just for fun do you? This is for real, Caroline. I love you. I love you and I'm going to marry you.'

'You've been in the sun too long.'

'All right, make a joke of it while you can. Let Richard's bank dazzle you. I have it on good authority that he won't inherit one little bit of the bank, anyway.'

'I'm not interested in money.'

'I apologise,' he said contritely. 'I shouldn't have said that. Can't you understand that the little man doesn't let it happen to just one person? That would be too cruel.'

'What little man?' she asked perplexed.

'Cupid, of course. The little fellow with the bow and arrows.'

'Oh stop being silly.'

'Now you're talking like Lady Caroline. I much prefer plain Caroline.'

'I must go,' she said making a move, but his hand covered hers and she hesitated.

'No,' he told her. 'We haven't had our second pot of tea yet. I shouldn't have told you all this so soon after your engagement. It will take you a week or two to realise your mistake. Only, if you find me staring at you like some goopy fish out of water, you will know why. I'm not out of my mind. On the contrary I think I've just come to my senses. More tea?'

She blinked at this abrupt change of subject while he gestured to a passing waitress who took one look at him and forgot the order she had just taken. He had that sort of personality. He ordered more tea and sat back and smiled at Caroline.

'If I didn't know you didn't drink, I'd say you'd been at the bottle,' she grumbled.

'I have. The one marked 'love potion'. What's the matter Caroline? Don't you like being loved? Shall I jump off a mountain or run under a train for you? Say the word and it is as good as done.'

'If you think I believe a word you're saying, you insult my intelligence.'

'All right. Let's change the subject for the moment. It will keep.'

She flushed under his amused stare. In a way she rather liked his banter, but it was lamentably un-English. Nobody had ever spoken to her like that, least of all Richard who alone had the right. She wondered if Magnus did it to all the pretty girls he met.

'I suppose you realise that we know

nothing about you.' She said it impulsively and regretted it almost at once.

'Meaning what?' he asked quietly.

'We don't even know you work for Laker & Day. We have only your word for that. My father took you very much on trust.'

'Yes he did. Well, tomorrow is Monday. You can ring them up and ask.'

'I'm sorry, I've no doubt you do work for them. It's just that — well you're a total stranger and not only are you making free with our library, which can't do much harm anyway, but you're being pretty forthright with me. You don't even know me, Magnus.'

'Know you? Of course I know you. You're the girl I love.'

'I wish you'd stop saying that. It doesn't impress me.'

He waited while tea was served again, and then when she had poured he smiled gently.

'I'm not trying to impress you. Shock you perhaps; impress you, no. I don't

106

have much to impress you with, other than a middling good job here in England, and an American small town background of which I am very fond and not at all ashamed. I often wish I were back in Putney, Vermont. I don't think I'd swap it for your stately home, Caroline — but I love you and I wanted to say so. I guess you might say I was embarrassed and tried to brazen it out by being outrageous.'

'I wish you'd just do whatever it is Daddy wants, and leave me alone.'

'All right,' he agreed unexpectedly. 'If that's what you want, I shan't refer to the matter again. You can't stop me loving you, but I'll stop mentioning it. I suppose Richard is coming back tonight, is he?'

'No, not this week. He usually eats with us on a Sunday night, but he can't this week.'

'That's a small mercy. Right now I don't like him very much. After tea I shall get back to the library.'

'Are you staying to supper?' she asked.

'I think your father half expects me to, but the answer is no. I'm a little bit disorganised. I haven't seen much of my flat this weekend so far. I have a few chores to catch up with which I ought to have done yesterday, plus the fact that it's shampoo night and I have things to get ready for the cleaners. Also I have some food in the fridge that will go bad. I really do have to go back.'

She nodded and rather astonishingly felt just a tiny tinge of disappointment.

'However,' he grinned, 'I expect I'll be round again on Tuesday or Wednesday.'

Later when he had gone she and her father sat together having a chat before supper.

'What do you think of young Manisty?' Vivian asked her.

'He seems — capable.'

'Ah, that's the word. Capable. He does, doesn't he? He's got lots of fantastic ideas. I only hope that some of them work.'

'Why?' Caroline asked. 'Aren't we doing well?'

'We're doing very well, all things considered, but I would like to make the most of this place. It's all I've got to leave you.'

'You sound like an old man. You're only fifty-six. You'll be here for years and years.'

'I hope so,' he agreed. 'I'd like to. Still, as I say, this is a sort of family business now. Funny, I was brought up to do nothing. My father left me what looked like a reasonable sum of money and it all went up in smoke. Death duties. Still we have a fairish income, enough for us both, and the extra income from our paying visitors will cover you against the grasping bureaucrats who will gather round like vultures when my time comes to push off and join our ancestors.'

'I wish you'd stop talking about dying.'

'Of course. I was really talking about Manisty. Interesting young fellow. Remind me to telephone Jack Day tomorrow morning, however.'

'Don't worry, I shan't forget,' Caroline assured him, and meant it.

5

Lisette Taylor had that slim boyish figure and the large expressive eyes so loved by those who pay models to pose in their wildly expensive clothing. She had a pixie face and short fair hair which framed her head in two heavy wings. Her make-up was always flawless, and she gave the impression of someone whose hands were never dirty. This was slightly misleading for she was a do-it-yourself fiend and had transformed what had been a pleasant flat into something quite extraordinary.

When you saw her, as was very frequently the case, on the glossy expensive front cover of *Haute Mode* or *Her Ladyship*, you could be excused for thinking that she was just a pretty face — with, of course, equally pretty adjuncts. In fact she was a very determined and positive personality, highly intelligent and well-informed, and earned the sort of money most young girls dream of and most models despair of. She was not particularly pleased to find Magnus Manisty on her doorstep but she was polite.

'Hullo Magnus, come in.'

He followed her inside and sat down without invitation.

'What is it you want?' Lisette demanded.

'There's no need to go on being mad at me. Can't we be friends?'

'Last time I saw you I told you to drop dead,' she replied. 'I didn't mean it. What I meant was go away and don't come back. I'm sorry Magnus, but whatever there was between us is finished.'

'All right,' he agreed equably. 'I understand. However I have a little business to discuss which might possibly interest you. It concerns a young sprig of the nobility and a camera.'

Lisette stared at him for a moment and then sat down facing him.

'Fire ahead,' she suggested looking interested.

Magnus's business did not take long and when they had settled the immediate details she got rid of him, for on Monday nights she invariably did the weekend chores she was always far too busy to take care of at weekends. Tonight, however, she made a mug of coffee and sat and thought about Magnus's visit. It sounded interesting. If this Richard Verney really could use a camera, and really was going to be the 7th Baron Binfield then there were distinct possibilities. Anyway Magnus had promised to pay her a professional fee for posing for Richard Verney on Saturday, so if the whole thing turned out to be a waste of time she would have some money to console her.

She was more interested in Richard Verney's potential than the money, however, and she drank her coffee and speculated on what the outcome of it all might be. She had known Magnus long enough to know that he was very determined and accustomed to getting things done. If he had decided to turn the heir to the Binfield barony into a successful photographer — and for some mysterious reason it seemed that he had — then there was every chance that he would manage it splendidly.

Magnus meantime was behaving in an uncharacteristic manner. Having settled his little bit of business with Lisette exactly as he had planned to settle it, he went straight home, shed his suit, climbed into a pair of light-weight summer slacks and a towelling shirt, and sat in the window seat of his flat with a book. On the face of it this was fairly routine. Young publishing executives spend much time yacking in their offices and frequently carry off books and manuscripts to read at home where they won't be interrupted. Magnus had a theory, one which did not much amuse his starchy chairman, that if they closed the London office and did all the work at home and by post, they could do a year's work in three months.

This evening however the volume he was reading with bated breath was not one of the splendidly produced English Heritage Series, or the more widely distributed English Nooks and Crannies Series, or even one of the new Battles, Churches and Monuments Series. It was *Antiquarian Miscellanea* and he re-read pages 413–431 at least ten times, and then made a few notes of things to chase up in the library. If The Rev. Wilkins Welbeck, M.A., D.D., had been even approximately sober when he wrote these significant pages, then life at Portcullis Manor was about to be transformed. It pleased Magnus that he would be doing the transforming.

He had his usual supper of yoghurt, rye crispbread, with cottage cheese, and his own favourite brew of tea blended for him by Skryke's in St. James's Market who had been purveying special blends to the discriminating classes for two centuries or more. He showered early, did his rhythmic deep breathing exercises, and went to bed much earlier than usual.

It was a busy week for him, for he had several irons in the fire at once, and when he went to Portcullis on Tuesday and Wednesday, to look up some books and chat to Vivian Eaton, he seemed much preoccupied. This did not stop him from staring at Caroline as though he was a hungry cannibal with a yen for blonde steaks, but he missed at least two opportunities to tell her how nice she looked.

At eleven o'clock on Saturday morning Richard Verney arrived in his little yellow sports car and sought out his fiancée. He pecked at her cheek dutifully, and then asked, 'Have you seen that fellow Manisty, darling?'

'No,' she answered. 'Why are you carrying your camera round your neck Richard? Are you going to take my photograph or something?'

'What? Oh this. Well, don't you know? I'm photographing someone Manisty is bringing.'

'Of course I don't know. Nobody has told me a thing. Who is this somebody and why are you photographing him?'

'It's a her, not a him. A model. Manisty has an idea about my becoming a fashionable portrait photographer or something. I told you.'

'You did nothing of the sort, you mean pig. When did this happen?'

'Last Sunday. I wonder if he was serious. I don't want to lug my camera about all day.'

'Then take it off and put it down on a table. Who is this model?'

'I honestly don't know darling. Someone he knows.'

He did his best to explain the situation to her until they were interrupted by the arrival of Magnus and Lisette. As Magnus introduced his erstwhile girlfriend, Caroline scowled and Richard gaped. Lisette was dazzling this bright day, and made Caroline feel like a frowsy spinster at a Church social. Caroline recognised Lisette of course, for she frequently read the glossy super-magazines in which Lisette was prominently featured.

Magnus, who was accustomed to Lisette's traffic-stopping appearance, quickly got rid of her and Richard.

'You take him outside honey and prop yourself against a battlement and let him do his worst. You'll have to arrange your own poses. I want really high class stuff, remember. You're an expert after all.'

'Just like that?' Lisette demanded.

'How else?' Magnus asked reasonably. 'Richard has had no experience. I'm sure he'll do exactly as you tell him.' Richard nodded dumbly and followed Lisette from the room.

'What *is* all this?' Caroline asked suspiciously.

'I'm trying to help your betrothed to earn a few fast dollars. I gather he hasn't too much in the way of financial expectations. Hasn't he told you?'

'He was just telling me when you came. How do you come to know Lisette Taylor? She's a top model.'

'So she's always telling me. We met.'

'She's not the one you had a row with, is she? Last weekend?'

'She is as a matter of fact,' he admitted. 'There was nothing serious between us — not like it is with you,' he assured her.

'There is nothing whatever between us!'

'There will be,' he promised. 'About Lisette, we are just good friends. You may quote me. She's just the person who can help Richard. If he takes some decent shots I think I can set him up in business. You see I have friends. One is a television reporter and the other is a feature writer on *The Daily World*. I have prepared a press release all about your precious Richard, the heir to an ancient barony, and his velvet and mink lined studio at the ancient family seat, Verney Hall, on the Thames near Weybridge.'

'It isn't on the river at all.'

'Don't interrupt me with details which are irrelevant. I have it all written. Baron's heir aspires to become portrait photographer for ordinary people. You too can have your own private Cecil Beaton at reasonable prices. All I need are some very good examples of his work. Of course if people get the idea that the noble pile in the background of the photograph is Verney Hall, so much the better.'

'Verney Hall is an excrescence,' Caroline exclaimed. 'It isn't even remotely like Portcullis.'

'I guessed as much. What of it? Nobody will actually say where Lisette was photographed. I think I can get Richard on TV, and after that his fortune is made — provided always that he really can work that Rolleiflex of his properly.'

'He's very good.'

'I'm glad to hear it. It is important. You can get away with murder provided that when the time comes you deliver the goods. This is just a small exercise in sales promotion. Your Richard is the product and I am promoting him.'

'Why?' she demanded.

'Because he asked for help,' Magnus answered without a blush. 'Obviously I couldn't hold out any hope of his beating the Duke of Bedford in the stately home racket — sorry, business. I must remember to stop calling your profession a racket. So I asked a few cunning questions, discovered that he will one day be a bold baron and that he takes snaps of shadows, drains and puddles, or whatever it is he finds artistic merit in, and there we are.'

'I don't see where that girl comes in.'

'My dear Caroline, that is the master stroke. We promoters have to have our valuable contacts. Remember the golden words of success. It isn't who you know that counts, but who knows them. Lisette is doing this as a favour to me, but the people who will see the photographs and the press release won't know that. They will simply see that the top model in Britain models for this upper-class shutter-snapper, and assume that he must be the very hottest thing in the 'say cheese' business. You'll be lucky if Richard even speaks to you a year from now, and you'll have to marry me after all. He'll be too busy taking photographs of the wedding to bother about the responses.'

'So that's it,' she said acidly. 'You're up to something, aren't you?'

'I am?' He looked hurt. 'Just trying to give your penurious nobleman a helping hand. It's a cruel world. He isn't going to inherit Verney's Bank, so he'll want much more than the sort of salary those vultures will pay him. A girl like you deserves the very best.'

'You don't fool me.'

'I didn't think I did. That's one of the things I like about you.' He grinned widely. 'Now I must go and have a word with your father and then bury myself in the library again for an hour or two.'

'How are you getting on?' she asked, curiosity overcoming her just suspicions.

'Well, the book is going to be easier than I thought. I ought to be able to get the first draft done in three months or even less, then I simply tidy it up, have it decently typed, and that's that. I have a printer lined up already. As a matter of fact I think it deserves a better fate than to be sold here. I want to discuss that point with your father.'

'You're optimistic.'

'My business is books,' he smiled. 'Wouldn't it be nice if Laker & Day published it and it sold thousands of copies in bookshops?'

'Wait a moment,' she objected. 'You were going to write a manuscript for my father to have printed and to sell to tourists. He offered you a fee and you refused.'

'That's right,' Magnus admitted.

'Yes, but if you write some sort of best-seller you'll have the copyright or whatever it is. We wanted to make a little money out of the book, remember?'

'It won't be a best-seller,' he promised. 'All I thought was that it ought to sell in bookshops as well as at Portcullis

Manor. Anyway I'll put your name on it and you can have the royalties.'

'*My* name?'

'The Horrible Happenings at Portcullis Manor by Caroline Eaton. Or better still, Lady Caroline Eaton. It will sell on that alone. Do you mind?'

'Why should you do that?' she asked him.

'Why not? All I'm doing is helping you and your father a little. It's nothing much.'

'You really mean it?'

'You checked on me,' he asked with a grin. 'Surely you know I'm a sober citizen.'

'How did you know we checked?' she asked crossly.

'I was told. We're a gossipy lot at Laker & Day.'

'So it would seem.'

'Well, now you know I'm a young country boy of good character . . . '

'A young country boy? You? Don't make me laugh,' she scoffed.

'No harm in trying. At least I have a

good character. If you want to pay me for my labours let me wear your coronet to dinner one night.'

'I don't have one.'

'I'm deeply disappointed. I'd counted on seeing you in it. No ermine robes?'

'None at all.'

'Don't you drop in on the Queen for tea now and then?' he asked plaintively.

'Haven't even met her,' Caroline answered. 'I can't stand horses or corgis so I shouldn't think we'd have much in common.'

'How terrible. You're nothing but a fraud. You'll be telling me your father doesn't play polo.'

'He plays a nifty hand of poker,' she smiled. 'I believe he actually played in the Wall Game at Eton.'

'You're nothing but a bunch of peasants in disguise,' he said pleasantly.

'Nobody's denying it. I'd far rather be an upper class American with a private jet, three yachts at the landing stage and colour television in every car.'

'I suppose we're as disappointing as

you are,' he remarked. 'Nothing is what it seems in this cruel and hard world. I must go and see your father anyway. I suppose he really is an earl?'

'Don't you know? Didn't you check on us?' she asked impishly.

'I did. He is. Does *he* have a coronet?'

'We have a very old one which is kept in a bank vault. I believe it is quite valuable. At the coronation he hired one.'

'This is a plebeian age. Baked beans and sliced bread have been the ruin of Western civilisation. Hiring coronets indeed. I wonder if there's any money in it,' he concluded thoughtfully. 'Hiring coronets and things, I mean. The capital outlay must be ferocious. Well, you'd better keep an eye on Richard. Lisette has turned stronger heads than his.'

'Richard is engaged to me,' Caroline retorted.

'Yes, but it won't do any harm to put in an appearance. Sort of remind him, you know.'

'Oh, you . . . ' She glared as he slopped out of the room, and then she grinned. However she followed a moment later to look for the errant Richard.

★   ★   ★

The rose garden at Portcullis was rather neglected by the visitors to the house and grounds, for it was not at all exciting. However it did have one of the best views of the house itself as well as some rather lovely roses. Richard led Lisette to it and she nodded approvingly.

'Yes, it's a good setting,' she agreed.

'Do you really think so?' He was pleased.

'Of course. What sort of experience have you had of photography?'

'Oh this and that,' he said vaguely. 'I don't photograph people as a rule. Manisty said I ought to.'

'Really.' She digested this. 'I tell you what, you pose for me.'

'I beg your pardon?' he asked, taken aback.

'I'll set you up in the pose, and then we simply change places. All right?'

'I suppose so.'

'If you'd stand over there with that angle beside you — this is colour film isn't it?'

'Colour film — ? Good lord no. I never use it.'

'What does that mean?' she demanded.

'Any fool can take a colour photograph. You set the knobs and you either get it right or wrong. Nothing in between. There's no scope in colour photography. I prefer to take good black and white photographs. I like to play with light and shade.'

'I see. Well that's different. I mean we don't have to trouble about the colour of the roses, do we?'

'Not at all.' He hesitated. 'What's it like to be famous? I hear you're the most famous model in England.'

'Britain,' Lisette corrected. 'You soon get used to it. Modelling is just a job.'

128

'Some job,' he said admiringly.

'You want to keep your mind on your work,' she warned. 'Are you really going to be Lord Somebody?'

'Lord Binfield. Yes. I'm my uncle's heir. I shall be the 7th baron. It's not terribly important.'

'I should think it's rather fun being a lord.'

'I wouldn't know. I've never been one,' he confessed. 'My father was an Hon., but it didn't bring him much luck. He had rather a lot of girlfriends but he lost all his money.'

'Do you want to be a professional photographer?' she enquired.

'If there's money in it, I suppose I do. I never really thought about it. I like photography. I spend hours in the dark room trying to produce interesting prints.'

'That's a good sign. Move over to the left.'

She manoeuvred for position and then put the camera on the ground.

'All right, you stay there.' She came

over and joined him and gave him a quick smile. 'Silly isn't it?' she laughed. 'Never mind, it's all in a good cause. Now you go and pick up the camera and take a couple of shots of me here.'

He did as she asked, using different settings and taking four photographs altogether. They moved on to another suitable spot.

'I say,' he remarked, 'try this. What do Christian Dior, Vivien Leigh and Casanova have in common with Uncle Walter and Charlie's Aunt? Do you know?'

Lisette shook her head. 'I can't imagine. What do they have in common?'

'They're all roses of course.'

'I see.'

'I made that up myself,' he told her proudly.

'Who'd have thought it. Are you some sort of amateur gardener?'

'I often photograph flowers, especially roses. In black and white of course. I've got rather a super enlargement of one taken against the light. It turned out terrifically. My best photograph is of a boot beside a dustbin.'

'You did say a boot beside a dustbin didn't you?' she asked wonderingly.

'Yes.' He waxed enthusiastic. 'You see the point? The poignancy? The untold pathos of the composition. It got a prize, a first as a matter of fact.'

'Did it really? You must find photographing me rather dull.'

'Oh no,' he exclaimed.

'Unless of course you think I resemble a boot in some way.'

'Most certainly not,' he yammered.

'Or perhaps the dustbin?'

'Did I say something wrong? I'm most fearfully sorry. All I meant was . . . well, I don't know what I meant. I'd far rather photograph you any day.'

'I hope so,' Lisette sniffed, her eyes glinting with satisfaction. He was such a nice, tame little lord-to-be.

'I mean, it's an honour to photograph you.'

She wondered if he realised just how true that was. Lots of people wanted to photograph her but were denied the pleasure. They took several more photographs and then she asked idly, 'I suppose you know this place rather well. You live in Weybridge don't you?'

'Yes, I expect Manisty told you. I know Portcullis very well indeed. Caroline and I are engaged.'

'I beg pardon?' she asked bleakly.

'I said we're engaged. Lady Caroline Eaton — you met her when you arrived.'

'I know who you mean. When did this happen?'

He saw nothing odd in the question. 'Last weekend. Of course it's been sort of settled for years.'

'I see. How cosy. I wonder why you want to be a photographer if you're going to acquire all this for yourself, or has she a brother who'll inherit?'

'No, no brothers. Caroline is the only child. One wants to do something. I can't live off my wife's paying visitors, can I?'

'No? About last weekend, I wonder

why Magnus didn't tell me.'

'Probably didn't think it would interest you. She's a splendid girl.'

'Yes. Let's try over there, shall we?' Lisette did not wish to hear anything about Caroline Eaton.

They were trying over there when Caroline found them.

'Hi,' Richard called, catching sight of her out of the corner of his eye. 'Come to watch the fun?'

'Yes,' Caroline answered, coming up to him. 'How's it going?'

'Splendidly. I think some of these ought to be rather good. I'm trying out a new film that should give me really superb enlargements. I'll be up all night making enlargements. Jolly interesting. I never realised that the human figure could be so fascinating.'

'You don't say.' Caroline gave him a chilly stare.

'Look, you may want to stay up all night but I don't,' Lisette called waspishly. 'I'm tired of holding this pose for you.'

'Oh dear, sorry. Em . . . ready?'

'Ready. Shoot.'

She turned on a natural, relaxed smile and Richard dutifully clicked, clicked and clicked again. Then he looked up and nodded. 'Those were good. You're an absolute genius at picking the right spot to photograph.'

'I have had a little practice in being taken.'

'Marvellous. I could do this all day.'

'We should try some indoor ones.'

'Good idea,' he exclaimed. 'We'll shoot off this film first, and then I've got a fast one. We'll use the octagon room between crocodiles.'

'What?' Lisette asked.

'Crocodiles. Long crocodiles of paying members of the public winding in and winding out again. There's always about ten minutes or more between them.'

'Good.'

'Perhaps I'd better go,' Caroline remarked huffily.

'Oh no,' Richard protested. 'I was just telling Lisette we were engaged.

Wasn't I Lisette?'

'You were,' Lisette agreed dead pan.

'Were you?' Caroline echoed. 'I'm sure that fascinated Miss Taylor.'

Richard gazed from one to the other, puzzled. Such stunning girls. What on earth was wrong? Had he put his foot in it somewhere? He could not think how he could have. He'd been too busy photographing.

'Why not keep us company?' Richard asked gallantly.

'I'm not sure I want to, but yes, perhaps I ought to keep an eye on you.'

'As long as we can get a move on,' Lisette interrupted cattishly. 'I haven't got all day.'

'Aren't you staying for lunch?' Richard demanded, astonished.

'Nobody invited me. Anyway I don't particularly want to stay. I don't like crowded places.'

'Well, there's a marvellous little place on the river about two miles away. It's called 'The Spinner'. The food is superb. Why don't we make up a threesome?'

'You know I can't come out for lunch today, Richard,' Caroline reminded him.

'Oh dear, nor you can.'

'Too bad,' Lisette sympathised. 'You're sure you can spare your fiance, Lady Caroline?'

Both Richard and Caroline stared. This was a move they had not anticipated. Lisette herself had no idea what made her say it except that she did not much like Lady Caroline Eaton. Caroline had Portcullis Manor. Why couldn't she leave the sweet little lordling alone?

'Well, er,' Richard managed a smile. 'Caroline will probably be busy anyway, won't you darling? After all, the very least I can do for Lisette is to take her to lunch. She's a professional model and this *is* her day off.'

'Oh quite,' Caroline said with a little laugh. 'I shall be far too busy to miss you, Richard. You get on with your snapping or whatever it is and take Miss Taylor out to eat. I'll see you tomorrow.'

'Tomorrow?' he asked.

'You'll want to get to your darkroom won't you?'

'I do rather,' he agreed nodding. 'Yes indeed. I can hardly wait.'

'I thought so. Well, don't let me stop you.'

She gave them a haughty look and marched off. Lisette suppressed a triumphant little smile. That was a clear victory for her in round one. It was turning out to be a far more amusing day than she had thought it would.

6

'Daddy,' Caroline said after dinner one evening, 'do you think I'm a fool?'

'What an odd question my darling,' Vivian Eaton answered, raising his eyebrows elegantly. 'Of course not. Who said you are? I'll horsewhip the scoundrel.'

'Nobody, but ... Well, Richard spends more and more time with that awful photographic model.'

'Those were lovely photographs he took.'

'She didn't have to go to Verney Hall with him to watch him do the printing and enlarging, did she? And anyway her part in it is done.'

'That was a splendid write-up he got in the press, and then the bit on television too. He's doing well.'

'He's only been at it a month,' she snapped and then sighed. 'I'm sorry. I shouldn't be taking it out on you. He's gone to see her tonight. At her flat in Putney.'

'Business I expect.'

'He's supposed to be photographing fat businessmen and their smug wives at twenty-five or thirty pounds a click. Not hobnobbing with the highest paid model in the business. I wonder if I'm not too tolerant.'

'You don't think there's anything going on do you?' her father asked, pouring more coffee.

'No,' she said slowly. 'Richard isn't the sort. I mean, if there were he'd come and tell me. I bet he confessed to everything at school. Daddy, do you like Richard?'

'What an odd question.' The seventh earl considered his prospective son-in-law. 'He's all right I suppose. A bit unenterprising, but now that Magnus has set him up as a photographer I daresay he'll do all right.'

'Do you want him as a son-in-law?'

'I don't *want* him,' Vivian protested.

'I could manage without him. I thought you loved him.'

'So did I,' she sighed. 'I was quite sure of it. Now I don't know. He's a drip.'

'Yes, well I wouldn't have said that myself but I'm damned if I'll argue with you. He is. Lots of people are. At least he's harmless.'

'He's not like Magnus.'

'Not in the least like him. I wonder what Magnus is up to.'

'Is he up to something?'

'Oh yes. It's very hush hush. It's a big surprise for us.'

'I wonder what it can be. Is it the book?'

'I don't think so. No, it can't be that. He's only halfway through it. What a splendid chap he is. Full of go. Nothing about him surprises me. I'm amazed he doesn't own Laker & Day by now.'

'I wish he'd never brought Lisette Taylor here. She's twisting Richard round her little finger.'

'Perhaps there's some good reason for it.'

'I can't think what it can be. He's not a fashion photographer. He won't even take a colour photograph. He's certainly got off to a good start with this new idea of Magnus's, but that wretched girl doesn't come into it at all.'

'Do you think she's trying to cut you out?' her father asked interestedly.

'I don't know,' Caroline sighed. 'I honestly don't know. I just know that he sees far too much of her. I'll tackle him about it tomorrow.'

'Do that. Oh, and Magnus will be here tomorrow evening early.'

'Why?'

'Something to do with that surprise of his. He specially asked me to be at home — not that I go about much these days. I prefer it here. We ought to take Magnus out to dinner you know.'

'I can't think why. He eats here about four times a week at the very least.'

'That's not the same thing at all. If I'd paid someone to do this writing it would have cost me hundreds, and he's busy working on that time museum idea too. Of course, it won't affect us this year, but it should open next May. Then there's the Eaton Collection. I'm rather pleased about that. We've got permission to put up a small building near the car park, among the trees there. I don't care if it loses money. I like the idea of it. The Eaton Collection, eh?'

'I know Magnus has you eating out of his hand.'

'Why not?' her father asked. 'What a decent fellow he is. Nobody asked him to help. He doesn't get paid. Surely we can take him out to 'The Coxswain's Cabin' next Saturday? Have a real blow-out.'

'It's so expensive. It's fantastic.'

'I know. We can afford it and who better to take than Magnus? Bring Richard too, of course.'

'Ha. If he's free. We'll see,' Caroline said darkly.

She saw Richard sooner than she expected for he drove up that very evening after ten. She let him in and offered him a drink.

'No thanks. I stopped off to see how you are. I've been to Putney.'

'Yes I know.'

'Lisette has the most marvellous idea. She's going to do what they call a 'spread' for *Elegance*, which is one of those enormous expensive glossy magazines.'

'I know it.'

'Yes, well she's doing it at Verney Hall, and I'm going to be featured in it. Sort of combined operation sort of thing. She's fixed it with the other people. It will be good publicity for me, and we're going to work on someone called Edgar Teagarden.'

'Who on earth is he?'

'A client of mine. Don't you see, people will think that if they come to me for their portrait they're liable to bump into Lisette and maybe even get photographed with her. It's fabulous.'

'What's in it for her?'

'Nothing. What an odd question.'

'Darling, Lisette Taylor is a professional at the top of a very tough and demanding profession. Why should she bend over backwards to help you? Do you pay her?'

'Pay her? Certainly not. I wouldn't insult her.'

'*Couldn't* is the word, darling. Not *wouldn't*.'

'I say, that's not fair.'

'Something funny is going on. Look here, are you tired of me Richard?'

'No darling. What a silly question. I'm engaged to you.'

'You see more of that wretched girl than you do of me.'

'That's only because I've been starting up in business. We're just good friends. One of her chums is selling me some super equipment at a really keen price. Secondhand of course. She's terribly decent.'

'That's what bothers me,' Caroline sniffed.

'I can't think what's come over you. You aren't usually bitchy.'

'Well I like that. Who's bitchy?'

'Sorry but . . . '

'If you feel like that, Richard Vernon, you know what you can do with your engagement ring.'

'Hey, hold on. I didn't mean it. I just meant . . . well, you *are* jolly hard on Lisette. She's done so much for me darling, and well, it's for us both in the long run.'

'She may be doing it for you,' Caroline said darkly, 'but don't you fool yourself that she is doing anything for me. The horrible snob.'

'What?'

'I know a snob when I see one. I bet if you weren't your uncle's heir she wouldn't even speak to you.'

'That's a ridiculous thing to say. You're the snob.'

'Me?' Caroline gaped. 'You're mad. I don't give a hoot about things like that.'

'Neither does Lisette.'

'That for a tale,' she snorted.

'I'd better go and come back when you're in a good mood.'

'If you're going to continue to be insulting you'd better not come back at all.'

Richard gave her a despairing look and fled. Sometimes he thought rather incoherently as he got into his car and roared off, women were very peculiar. Except for Lisette — she was a real pal.

Caroline meantime considered whether or not she should telephone him as soon as he got home. She had been unnecessarily sharp. Common sense told her not to show weakness. She was the injured party. Richard was not behaving as a well-brought up fiance ought to behave. Let him stew for a bit.

The following morning the telephone rang shortly after they had finished breakfast, and Caroline got up to answer it.

'Portcullis Manor,' she announced.

'Who is speaking please?'

'Lady Caroline Eaton.'

'Good morning.' The voice became effusive. 'This is Filsom Faulkner here. Mr. Manisty of Laker & Day said it would be all right to telephone you.'

Caroline started. Filsom Faulkner was a household name in the television world, and his programme *With Faulkner* had one of the top ratings.

'Er yes?'

'Can I bring a crew round this afternoon about two? Will that be convenient? And will Lord Thornbury be at home?'

'Yes,' she said dazed. 'We'll all be here. What is all this?'

'We're doing a programme on the family. Hasn't Mr. Manisty told you?'

'No.'

'He will. It's about his discovery. Now you don't have to worry about a thing. We'll look after all the details but I'd like to shoot it today for this evening's show. It's quite a remarkable discovery. I expect you're delighted.'

'Oh thrilled,' Caroline agreed wondering what on earth he was talking about.

'I suppose your father ought to be King of England. Of course we can't say that, but it's certainly an odd business. How do you feel about it?'

'Er . . . you know. We haven't quite got used to it.' That seemed a suitably non-committal answer. What on *earth* had Magnus been up to?'

'Two o'clock then? At Portcullis?'

'Certainly. Will there be many of you?'

'About six, and we'd like to do a feature for the *TV Times*. We'll pay our usual fee of course.'

'Surely.'

'Good morning then, Lady Caroline.'

Caroline hung up and stared bemused at the ivory coloured telephone.

'Who was it darling?' her father called.

'Filsom Faulkner. He's coming at two with a crew to do a programme on us.'

'The television chap? What for? What's happening?'

'Here's Magnus. We'd better ask him,' Caroline answered noticing the white Porsche drawing up in the drive.

A moment or two later Magnus erupted into the room.

'Hullo all. Sorry I'm late but I had to fix it with the office. Has Filsom Faulkner been on the telephone?'

'He has,' Caroline said grimly.

'Darn it. Sorry about that. I ought to have briefed you before, but I had such a lovely surprise planned and it all came unstuck. I had to beetle up to town, you see, and I got a flat tyre on the way here.'

'Tell us about it,' Caroline invited.

'How do I start?' Magnus looked round from Caroline to Vivian to Selina. He was very boyish in his exuberance and Caroline could not resist a smile. 'You know that book I borrowed — *Antiquarian Miscellanea*? Well I found an interesting story in it and I chased it up in one or two libraries. It seems to be probable enough, so I wrote it up and sent it off to Faulkner. It's gone to the *Daily Examiner* and the *Weekly Review* too, and I expect just about everybody will

149

pick it up. It's going to put Portcullis on the map. People will come here *before* nipping round to Buckingham Palace.'

'What is this all about?' Vivian asked bewildered.

'That octagon room of yours must have seen some merry times. You know Charles the Second had a son by Lucy Walter, and made him the Duke of Monmouth?'

They nodded.

'Thereby hangs a tale. The Good King Charles married Catherine of Braganza in 1664, a year *after* he made his illegitimate son a duke. According to my researches he didn't much like Catherine of Braganza and had a soft spot for darling Lucy. Now, according to the Reverend Wilkins Welbeck he *actually married* Lucy Walter, and Monmouth was *legitimate*. Of course it was a tricky situation and he had to marry Catherine subsequently, to keep up political appearances. About that time he took as mistress Frances Eaton, wife of the 9th Viscount Thornbury, and he and she frolicked here at Portcullis when nobody was waiting. She was a lady-in-waiting to Queen Catherine — although when she found any time to do any waiting is a bit of a mystery. Now the plot thickens.'

They were staring at him, mouths open and he grinned encouragingly.

'Catherine had a son. At that time the last thing Charles wanted was a son by her. He hoped that eventually he'd be able to recognise Monmouth as his heir. Remember he'd created him a duke only about eighteen months or two years before. So they told the queen that the baby was stillborn, and the baby was taken over by Lady Frances and her complaisant husband, and in due course succeeded as 10th Viscount — the son of King Charles II and Queen Catherine of England. Your own ancestor. It's all buried in the middle of that huge indigestible tome of Welbeck's with the headline in small print — 'The Truth About England's Royal Heir or the Mystery of King

Charles II.' You can read it for yourself.'

'That can't be true,' Vivian objected.

'It can, you know. I've known about this for a week or two and I've been chasing it up. Of course I can't prove, nor can anyone, that Charles and Lucy Walter really were married and in any event Monmouth got his head chopped off later on, when he tried to grab the throne by force. However the bit about the baby seems pretty well documented. Put it this way, there's supporting evidence that a switch was made. It's in the British Museum. It might not stand up in a court of law, and I doubt if they'd give the present tenants of Buckingham Palace notice on the strength of it, but equally well nobody can deny the facts with any certainty. It's really going to put this place on the map and by the time television and the press have finished with you you'll have had about a million pounds worth of first class national advertising. I've also sent the thing off to an acquaintance in New

York and I'll be surprised if it isn't all over the U.S.A. in no time at all.'

'You can't write things like that,' Vivian objected aghast.

'Why not?' Magnus asked, puzzled.

'It's disloyal.'

'It's true. What's disloyal about it? What's more, I believe that the 10th Viscount knew about it, for he was very anti-Stuart. Remember how you got your earldom, for raising a private troop of horse to fight Bonnie Prince Charlie? During the march on Derby, the then Lord Thornbury undertook the defence of the approaches to London, and when the rebels turned back he joined up with Cumberland. That's how you got your promotion. Why so anti-Stuart all of a sudden, and so pro-Hanover?'

'We always did like the party in power,' Vivian murmured.

'Maybe. Anyway I've sold a bill of goods to Filsom Faulkner and the editors of several journals, and I've found supporting documents in the British Museum. You'll have the other owners of stately homes closing up shop in disgust. They'll never be able to compete with this.'

'I always knew it,' Aunt Selina said calmly.

'You *what*?' Vivian and Caroline demanded simultaneously.

'I remember once our grandmother reprimanding me, Vivian. 'Behave yourself properly child,' she said. She was a very fierce old woman. 'Behave yourself properly, because you have royal blood in your veins.' It always puzzled me because she was a Druse, and there was nothing royal about them. They had two baronetcies and that's all. Now I understand. She must have known the truth.'

'First I ever heard of it,' Vivian snorted. 'I don't believe a word of it. Charles always wanted an heir. I read it in a history book.'

'Don't you see,' Magnus explained patiently, 'he thought he *had* one in Monmouth, and he didn't want another who might usurp Monmouth's claim?

Later on when Monmouth rebelled it was too late to tell the truth. Monmouth was made a duke in 1663, the marriage with Catherine was in 1664 and the bogus 10th Viscount was born in 1665. All long before Monmouth's rebellion. So officially Charles had no heir at all when he chopped off Monmouth's head.'

'Then why didn't he turn *us* into dukes or marquesses, instead of leaving us as mere viscounts?' Vivian asked.

'Ah, I thought of that too. I mean, they fairly flung titles around among their friends in those days, didn't they? The answer is simple. The 9th Viscount had a price for his silence. They would pretend the baby was theirs if Charles left his wife alone. The king agreed, but you don't really expect him to hand out any promotion after that, do you? I mean, he had to go and find another mistress, and even if it wasn't difficult it was probably a nuisance. It all fits in with everything else that's known. He stopped coming here soon after the baby turned up. I've brought Welbeck's book back and I've got a few other books in the car and a complete documentation of the research. I'll bring it in later. Any coffee Caroline?'

'Yes,' she said, her mind whirling. 'I'll ring for the maid.'

She did so. She was thinking that when it came to organising things, Magnus was in a class all by himself. He'd promised Vivian to help boost business. It looked as though he had just boosted it through the roof.

She looked at Magnus again, with something approaching awe in her eyes.

★   ★   ★

Filsom Faulkner and his henchmen had gone, winding up their cables and trundling away their trolleys and other equipment. Peace had settled once again on Portcullis — peace for the present, at any rate. Magnus was forecasting a record invasion on Saturday and talked of having a police cordon put round the house to control the crowds.

'Aren't you going to work today?' Caroline asked him.

'No. Nor tomorrow.'

'You've got two days off?'

'No.'

'What do you mean?' she asked. 'Don't be so cryptic Magnus.'

'I took my dictionary, my crocodile-leather covered notebook and my own private desk diary from the desk, and said goodbye to Laker & Day. I have quit.'

'Quit! Why?'

'I find the Heritage Series too deadly dull nowadays. I've decided to be a promoter. I'm promoting you right now.'

'You're doing that all right but you can't do it for ever,' she remarked.

'Well, I've had a quiet word with your father. I'm going to operate a bookshop in the grounds here. That will bring in a few pounds.'

'Not enough to live on.'

'Agreed. I have given some thought

to this living business. I've got a little bit of money in the bank. I don't really like work. Who wants to be a slave all his life? One only does it in order to eat. You admit that?'

'I suppose so,' she said uncertainly.

'Right, now we have identified our objective. To eat. The problem therefore is simply to find another way to get bread and occasional cake. I could of course establish an industry, but what good would that do? I don't want to end up as chairman of a giant corporation, jetting all round the world, feeding my ulcers on caviar, and watching my workmen go home happily in the evenings while I sit up worrying about how to hang on to my empire. That's worse slavery. The best way to get bread is to have a bread shop. Obvious.'

'You mean you're going to become a baker?' she asked, amazed.

'Goodness no. All floury and undignified. I shall open a little restaurant and call it 'The Drawbridge & Moat', charge exorbitant prices, try to get a liquor licence and see about running it as a night-club at nights. I shall cash in on your boom. I personally will continue to promote in a dignified way while other people work for me.'

'You hope.'

'I think I can get the premises, and with a bit of help from your father who is by the way of being a V.I.P. locally, I think I can get the necessary permits. Your father has said he'll do his best. I don't want to be rich. I've been wasting my time, commuting in the traffic to town every day. I'll buy a second-hand punt and laze on the river.'

'In winter?' she asked.

'In winter I shall buzz off to Austria and ski for four months.'

'That's going to be expensive.'

'No, I think I can fix it to be a tour operator's representative. That way I get a few perks.'

'You've got it all worked out, haven't you?'

'I've thought about it,' he agreed. 'I don't want to be chairman of Laker & Day, or any of its associated companies. I don't want twenty thousand pounds a year. Paying the tax on it would give me nightmares. I shall have fun. Something lucrative will turn up. One day I may go to Putney, Vermont, and take over my father's little store there.'

'Why the sudden change?' she asked, mystified. 'I thought you were going to be the successful Manisty.'

'I am, but not in the way I first thought. I still have my ambition of course.'

'What is it?' she demanded.

'Simple. Marry you.'

'Not that again please, Magnus. I'm engaged.'

'Um. I'm not impressed. You can't be serious and anyway from what I've heard Lisette has her hooks into Richard.'

He said this virtuously. It was none of his doing. He had put them together, suggested a few things to her in a purely business way, and sat back and watched the inevitable happen. If Lisette set her sights on Richard he was a dead duck, Caroline notwithstanding. It was not that Caroline wasn't ten times more attractive than Lisette, simply that Lisette in a determined mood was unstoppable and anyway Richard Verney had no backbone. Women would always be able to manipulate him. It was a compliment to Caroline that Lisette was less scrupulous.

He did not voice his thoughts. He simply smiled at her.

'Richard and Lisette have some sort of business arrangement,' she countered.

'I know,' Magnus nodded. 'Quite a good one too. If I were you, I'd drop him. He's not your type.'

'And you are?' she asked, amused.

'Why not? I have one unbeatable qualification.'

'Such as?'

'I'm in love with you. I think you are better than the entire female species wrapped up in a gold leaf and tied with diamonds and rubies. When we are old I shall push your wheelchair down to the water's edge and we shall sit hand in hand, watching the swans in the sunset. Isn't that poetic?'

'Swans on the river here?'

'Well who can say what it will be like when we're both a hundred?'

'Polluted,' she said absently.

'Magnus, you will say, fetch my shawl darling, it is growing chilly. And I'll hobble into the house, my saintly white head wobbling about on my shoulders like Little Noddy, and do your bidding. I shall love you just as much then as I do now.'

'You have a lurid imagination. I can't stand shawls.'

'How do you know what you'll be like at a hundred?' he asked reasonably. 'Caroline darling, get rid of Richard. Ditch him. Then we can get married. You'll be so rich you'll be able to pay somebody else to do all the work, and I'll have a manager in my little

162

bookstall, and we shall sit together in the tea garden watching all the customers churning up the lawn, holding hands under the table, drinking tea till it runs out of our ears.'

'You idiot.' She laughed. 'I refuse to take you seriously.'

'Your father likes me.'

'I'm not surprised. You've done a lot for him — not just this wild story about Charles the Second, but your other ideas, and you're working hard on that book about the house. Of course he likes you.'

'You don't?'

'I didn't say that,' she countered defensively.

'Then what do you say to this?'

He took her by surprise, gathering her in his arms and kissing her. For a moment she froze and then instead of struggling she discovered that she was kissing him back. It was enjoyable. It was very enjoyable indeed. His skin was smooth and he smelled nice.

'I love you,' he whispered and before

she could reply he was kissing her again.

When he stopped kissing her he held her gently by the elbows and looked into her eyes.

'Well?' he asked.

'I don't know. Don't ask me, Magnus.'

He saw the uncertainty in her eyes and dropped his hands to his sides. She was not a girl who could be pushed. He had given her something to think about and that was all he could hope to achieve at this stage.

'Now you know. I'm serious,' was all he told her as he moved away.

7

They had all watched the television programme last night, and now they read the big feature article in the *Daily Examiner*, each of them with their own copy at the breakfast table.

'You photograph nicely Caroline,' Selina commented, looking up. 'You were good on TV too.'

'Thank you Aunt Selina.'

'I say, it says I'm one of Britain's progressive peers here,' Vivian complained. 'What on earth do they mean by that? It sounds faintly indecent.'

'I think it's a general sort of compliment,' Caroline answered. 'It really means you're a sort of in-peer, not the sort they go gunning for. Lucky you don't hunt.'

'Can't ride,' Vivian remarked simply. 'Just as well these days. It costs a fortune. We're going to be busy tomorrow after all this publicity.'

'Wait till the *TV Times* article comes out,' Caroline laughed. 'And of course if the story really does go the rounds in America, we're made for life.'

'Is Magnus coming back this morning?' Vivian asked.

'He said just before lunch.'

'Good. I suspect it is going to be rather a frantic sort of day. Look at that concluding paragraph Caroline. Strong stuff. 'If Charles had been succeeded by his son, instead of his brother, James II, who can say how the course of history might have been changed? The United States might now be a member of the Commonwealth like Canada and Australia, the history of Ireland would have been vastly different, and the present troubles in Ulster might never have happened, and even the First and Second World Wars might never have been fought' I say, that's stretching it a bit.'

'Not really. If you accept one *if* in history, if you change one little thing, then anything subsequent could be changed,' Caroline shrugged. 'You don't think there's any truth in the story do you Daddy?'

'I shouldn't think so.' Vivian frowned.

'I'm sure there is,' Selina averred stoutly.

'You've always been a romantic, Selina. Anyway what good does it do, stirring up these old stories? We're not going to set up in opposition to the Queen. I wouldn't have the wretched job at any price. No freedom at all. I expect it's just some old wives' tale that parson chappie dug up years ago and put in his book.'

'And the documents at the British Museum?' Caroline asked.

'They only prove somebody *claimed* the baby was farmed out. It's quite true that there was a story, but that doesn't mean the story itself was true. I shouldn't let it bother you.'

'It doesn't.'

'Good. I was about to say that it will help business and that's enough bonus for me.'

'I think we ought to be very proud to

belong to the Royal Family,' Selina said persistently.

'My dear,' Vivian pointed out, 'I'm not at all sure that the present incumbents will be anxious to include us in the family circle. Concentrate on what we have, not what we might have had.'

'Talking of that,' Selina said changing the subject abruptly. 'Did you see the play on television last night?'

She had a TV set in her bedroom and watched it avidly every night until the last programme was over.

'No. Why?'

'Well, there was this golf course — in America. San Francisco I think. They had lovely little things you put the golf clubs in, and then you sat in front and drove to the next tee.'

'Trolleys.'

'Yes but they went by themselves.'

'I've heard of them,' Vivian nodded. He didn't play golf either.

'Wouldn't it be rather nice to have some here?' said Selina.

'What for?' her brother asked.

'For people to get around the grounds.'

'Are they extensive enough?'

'I'm sure some people with children would hire a little bus like that.'

'She may be right,' Caroline cut in.

'I'll ask Magnus,' Vivian agreed. 'Of course they probably cost the earth and aren't an economic proposition, but we'll see what Magnus says. I suppose we could start off with one — for ourselves — and on visitors' days we could try hiring it out.'

'I'd like to have one,' Selina said eagerly. 'Sometimes I feel too stiff to walk much in the grounds but to be able to drive along quietly and stop when one wanted — I think they must be electric.'

'I'll look into it,' Vivian promised.

The rest of the morning was punctuated by telephone calls, and three reporters turned up on the doorstep. Vivian was wearying of the game by the time Magnus appeared on the scene, and said so.

'There's bound to be an initial reaction,' Magnus pointed out. 'It's a good sign. You can't have it both ways, sir. Fame brings its little problems.'

'I wish you'd stop calling me sir.'

'How about sire?' Magnus laughed.

'Ha, much better. Now how are things going?'

'The book is coming along nicely. I'm well into the eighteenth century now and going strong. I'm making passing references to this latest discovery but I'm not playing it up too much. What I thought was that I could put together a little booklet about it — 'The Mystery of King Charles II and Portcullis Manor', or something like that. Get it printed on art paper and sell it at fifty pence a copy. Use a few photographic blocks to make it look good. Treat it as a separate thing.'

'I don't want people saying that I'm claiming the throne of England,' Vivian protested.

'Don't worry about that. I shall be

careful to refer to it as a story and a legend, and to blame the pious Mr. Welbeck for starting it.'

'Do make sure it doesn't look as though I'm giving myself airs,' Vivian pleaded. 'I can't imagine what my friends would say if they thought I was going into business as a rival royal. I say, that's good. Rival royal. Anyway we don't want anything like that old business of the two popes, do we? I'm all for a quiet life.'

'Don't worry. You shall approve everything before it is printed, and nothing will be done without your consent.'

'Thank you,' Vivian said with dignity.

'Now, about the time museum. I've got a letter from Buckley of Insoles. He can get a number of good time-pieces for us. There's a list attached. It totals about four thousand pounds but Buckley says that as an investment it's fantastic as they are worth about six right now without appreciation. Once they go into a museum they'll double in value. The other thing is that he has managed to get the original model for the first atomic clock. We can't get the clock itself — couldn't afford it even if we could get it. But the model . . . That's just as good. It's like owning the prototype of Concorde, isn't it?'

'How much?' Vivian asked thinking of the four thousand already involved.

'Nothing. It would be a gift. Read the letter yourself. Of course it has to have a little plate saying *donated by* and all that. The other thing is that I think it might be an idea to take a trip to Switzerland and Germany and look for clocks. What I mean is this. Old clocks take time to collect and cost a lot, and some are already in collections. But what about picking out the very best of current sorts of clocks — not just chronometers but different *types* of clocks — and having a good selection of current experiments in timekeeping? And maybe some sort of futuristic sort of display? It would be worth a month or six weeks in Switzerland and

Germany, and of course it could go down as business expenses and come off your tax.'

'That's an idea.'

'Then I suggest you go up to town to see Buckley and get him to advise you. He's terribly knowledgeable. He's clock crazy. It was a piece of luck meeting him at Insoles. He'll advise you how to go about it. I think this time museum will help enormously. People will be talking about the Portcullis Time Museum the way they talk about the Rockford one.'

'I never heard of the Rockford one till you told me about it.'

'That's because you are English. Come to think of it, I never heard of it either till I happened to go to Rockford — but then I'm pretty ignorant,' Magnus pointed out with a disarming grin. 'We'll wangle it into the Tourist Board literature. Come to England, see the Changing of the Guard, visit the Portcullis Time Museum, inspect the Crown Jewels. Yes, we must get one ahead of the Crown Jewels.'

'What are you doing today?' Vivian asked.

'Well, between ourselves I'm taking the afternoon off. I have to pop into Walton about my little restaurant. I think I may just possibly be on to a good thing here. You see, with Portcullis being developed, plus all the publicity about you and King Charles the Second, Walton is going to see a lot of visitors — more than ever before. That makes it a really good site for a restaurant. I don't want a cheap joint. I'm going after the people with fat wallets. There are plenty of them about nowadays. You know, the £1 touch for grapefruit, and fifty pence for coffee. No table d'hôte and a fifteen per cent service charge plus a filthy look if you don't leave a handsome tip into the bargain. And wine at criminal rates. The thing is to buy some wine nobody has heard about — that way they can't compare prices with other places. Did you know there's a chap in Hampshire who produces a very decent white wine? I'm thinking of bidding for his entire output and selling it as a unique English wine at about five times what I pay for it . . . '

'My God,' Vivian exclaimed.

'You don't approve?' Magnus asked.

'On the contrary, I am amazed. How do you hear about these things?'

'The wine? There was an article about it in a motoring magazine I occasionally buy. I always cut out things like that. You never know when they'll be useful.'

'You must have a lot of cuttings.'

'No, just one big index book with cuttings between the leaves. Only things that catch my eye and seem unusual and possibly interesting. As a matter of fact, as you know, I don't drink wine. I can't think why people pay what they do for the stuff. It's part of the general racket. You induce people to do stupid things on the grounds that if they don't, other people will look down on them. In the old days when water was undrinkable and dangerous people drank equally undrinkable but safe wines and ales. It was a question of survival. Now it is a cult, and what ought to be grape juice selling at the same price as tomato juice is now somebody's *château* and costs the earth; and if you don't pretend to understand what difference it makes what year it is, you're regarded as a peasant. Ah me. I wish I owned a vineyard in the right part of France.'

'You're an extraordinary chap,' Vivian told him.

'I don't think so. I hate pretence. Well I must be off but I'll be back later if I may.'

'Of course. You'll have dinner with us, surely?'

'I'd like to.' Magnus winked and strode off.

Caroline just missed him and asked her father, 'Where's Magnus gone?'

'Into Walton. It's about that restaurant he's interested in. He'll be back.'

'Oh good.'

Vivian turned and looked at her keenly. There had been a certain fervour about the way she had said 'Oh good.' He smiled gentle approval.

They were interrupted at that point by the arrival of Richard and Lisette. Lisette wore a new little West End creation the price of which would have fed a large family for a month, but which in fact had cost her nothing. It had to go back of course, but meantime she attracted the maximum of attention, a situation so normal that if she failed to do so she at once became self-conscious. Caroline gave her an icy look.

'Hullo Caroline,' Richard greeted her. 'That was a fantastic story in the paper today. I missed the television programme last night.'

'I did try to telephone you,' Caroline said very clearly. 'I tried four times all told. You were not at home.'

'Well, as a matter of fact I intended dropping in here, but Lisette and I had a spot of business to attend to.'

Caroline turned slowly to Lisette and back to Richard 'Lisette and you?' she enquired frigidly. 'Business? At night?'

Lisette concealed a satisfied smile.

'That's right,' Richard said hastily, 'it *was* business. There's this chap who has a studio in Appletree Yard and he wants to sell a lot of bits and pieces . . . '

' . . . and he could only see you at night with Lisette,' Caroline completed the sentence for him.

'We had to have dinner of course, afterwards.'

'But of *course* darling. Lisette needs feeding.'

It was Lisette's turn to scowl. Caroline had a nice feminine figure, such as men of good taste and considerable distinction admire; if they have any sense, that is. Not too much, and not too little. Just exactly right; measured out to the last milligramme by some expert hand. Lisette had the beanpole look without which no girl can possibly hope to model, although on what principle nobody seemed to know. She was perhaps not Twiggy, but she was decidedly branchy, Caroline thought maliciously.

'It's nice of you to come here anyway,' Caroline continued giving her betrothed a sizzling stare. 'What can we do for you?'

'I came to see you of course.'

'Bringing Lisette?'

There was a little silence and Vivian slipped away. He feared that if he stayed he would begin to laugh and that would spoil it all.

'Lisette has been at the studio this morning and we had lunch, and naturally came together.'

'Your studio?'

'Of course.'

'At Verney Hall?'

'You know it is.'

'I haven't actually seen it,' Caroline observed.

'I've asked you several times,' Richard defended himself.

This was true. Photography bored

Caroline to tears, and studios were no substitute for stately homes.

'I've been busy. Well, do make yourselves comfortable. I have to go.'

'Oh I say . . . '

'I'm sure you can entertain one another.' She gave them a decidedly haughty smile and walked off.

'Oh lord . . . ' Richard began.

'Don't worry darling.' Lisette gave his arm a squeeze. 'You forget she's just discovered she ought to be Queen of England. It's bound to make her insufferable. Shall we go?'

'I think I ought to stay for a bit,' Richard said doubtfully.

'Then buy me tea, darling.'

He gave her a smile and thought how pleasant she was, and full of good ideas. It would be excellent to have a nice cup of strong tea and forget Caroline's prickliness. He hoped she wasn't going to keep that sort of thing up after they were married. He'd dearly like to talk to her about it, but he was too terrified to attempt it.

'Isn't it marvellous?' he said to Lisette, turning to a safe and beloved topic. 'I've got eight sittings next week. That's two hundred pounds plus.'

'I know. Richard dear, a lot of people will be coming to Portcullis Manor after all that publicity. I think you ought to have a big sign up somewhere in town.'

'A sign?'

'Not a poster. Something in a window somewhere. You could probably rent one and have a very nice, elegant card, beautifully inscribed, with purple and gold velvet curtains as a backdrop. Yes, I'll think up something. Leave it to me. It must be worded just right to attract people. We must cash in on the boom.'

'If you say so.'

He had implicit faith in her judgement. It was she who had persuaded him to take the professional name of Lord. Portraits by Lord sounded excellent, and Lisette was herself fairly resourceful and knew a Malayan princess who was a struggling model. She had a glorious title, and in borrowed finery she made a wonderful advertisement at a very modest fee. Her portrait with sonorous title appeared along with an enormous photograph of a middle-aged male model in a lounge suit. The impression at once created by this clever combination was that Lord, whoever he was (and one soon found out about that too), was good enough to photograph royalty but also photographed anyone with a well-pressed suit and clean collar. Which was exactly what Richard wanted them to think, and as he was a beginner in the business it was easy to get an appointment with him, and people were astonishingly willing to fork out twenty-five pounds for three full-plate copies of a single study, which was the lowest end of the scale of charges.

He had at last found his niche in the great gullibility game. He could produce a perfectly good full-plate portrait of himself for about thirty pence, which covered all the costs. Why people didn't do it themselves he could not imagine.

*   *   *

Caroline's frigid attitude towards Richard was at least fifty per cent sham. His hobnobbing with Lisette did not annoy her nearly as much as she pretended it did. She herself was preoccupied with Magnus, and now she went to her bedroom and sat in the window seat, from which she could get a good view of the grounds, and took stock of the situation.

If Magnus really loved her, and he certainly seemed sincere if slightly eccentric on the subject, and if he really wanted to marry her, then perhaps she ought to consider the idea more deeply. Perhaps what Richard got up to with Lisette was becoming irrelevant. There was no doubt about it, so far as she was concerned the tanned, fair-haired, husky and non-conforming personality of Magnus attracted her more than Richard's somewhat stereotyped character. Even Vivian seemed to prefer the American.

She did not reach any hard and fast conclusions, but when she eventually went back downstairs she had decided to keep an open mind on the whole question of Magnus and Richard. As a result when she saw Richard with Lisette she gave them a dazzling smile.

'Did you see that?' Richard exclaimed.

'Mmm,' Lisette responded. 'I wonder what's pleasing her?'

'I wish you and she were better friends,' Richard complained. 'You seem to be all edgy with one another. It makes me uncomfortable.'

'Don't worry my dear.' She put one hand over his. 'It doesn't matter. I don't expect we'll meet again anyway.'

'No?'

'No. After all, what am I doing here anyway? I only came to keep you company. I've seen quite enough of Portcullis Manor to last me a lifetime. I don't belong in the gaping-tourist set, sweetie.'

'Of course not.' The mere idea of luscious Lisette as a gaping tourist was ludicrous.

'So why would I be seeing her again? In fact I really ought not to see you either.'

'Why not?' Richard was alarmed.

'You're engaged to her. You haven't been spending much time with her recently, have you?'

'I've been busy. Dash it, I'm not often busy. It isn't my fault.'

'Nobody said it was your fault, Richard, but it does put me in an awkward spot. Your precious Caroline seems to think I'm trying to get you away from her.'

She laughed lightly and looked pensive.

'Oh,' he said at last with a little shrug. 'I don't think so. Are you trying to back out of our date for tomorrow?'

He had arranged to take a lot of photographs of her on the river next day. Indeed for someone who was photographed for a living, Lisette had recently shown a highly unusual liking for working after hours. Ostensibly it was put down to giving Richard experience in portrait photography under all conditions, and certainly it made good practice, but Lisette knew very well that it was unnecessary. Richard knew enough about photography to stand on his own two feet without her.

'I suppose I can't,' she answered doubtfully.

'No, you mustn't,' he insisted.

'Very well, but you must make your peace with her. You're so newly engaged.'

He nodded, wondering what had got into him. He did not normally act in a precipitate way and it had been precipitate of him to telephone Caroline late at night in order to propose. He ought to have thought it over as soon as the idea got into his head. That was what he generally did. He was very good at thinking things over.

'All right,' he agreed half-heartedly. 'I'll have a little chat with Caroline. Why don't we go now? I'll talk to her later.'

'Good idea,' Lisette agreed fervently. She had no real desire to linger at Portcullis.

Richard paid for the tea and they went off, Lisette holding his arm. It was much later that one of the girls came to Caroline with an ostrich skin handbag.

'Oh Lady Caroline, this was handed in earlier. It was left by that young lady who was with Mr. Richard. They had tea together.'

'I know her.' Caroline held out her hand and took the bag. 'I expect she'll come back for it. If you see her before you go home, tell her I have the bag inside the house please.'

'Yes, Lady Caroline.'

Caroline admired the exterior of the expensive handbag and slipped it over her left wrist. She turned just in time to see Magnus's Porsche pull up in the car park. She walked slowly in that direction. He finished locking the door and then noticed her. His face split into a delighted grin.

'Hi,' he called. 'Not working?'

'Not today. How did things go for you?'

'All right.' He took her arm and they walked to the house. 'I settled one or two points. I thought I'd have an hour or so with some books, to check on a few little facts, get them dead right.'

'Come and have a drink.'

'With pleasure. Anything that interferes with work is good so far as I'm concerned. Especially if it concerns you.'

She flushed a little but said nothing in reply. She sent for a jug of ice-cold lemonade and they sat down together.

'I'm moving,' Magnus told her.

'Moving where?'

'About half a mile away near that road junction. It's called 'Peony Cottage' which is pretty awful, but the place itself is nice.'

'Why did you want to do that?'

'For one thing it's cheaper, and I get no salary cheque from now on; and much more important, it's near to you. I shall only want it for six months so it's ideal.'

'What happens in six months?'

'We'll get married before then.'

'You'll never go hungry if asking can get you food, will you?'

'I hope not,' he grinned. 'What's the matter?'

She was looking all around.

'Where did I put that handbag?' she asked. 'Did you see?'

'On the window ledge.'

'Oh good. It isn't mine.'

'I wondered why you were carrying one.'

'Your friend Lisette left it in the tea garden after she and Richard had tea.'

'Don't call her my friend in that tone of voice, as though I were in some way responsible for her,' he laughed. 'I never see her nowadays.'

'That's because she's with Richard.'

'Yes, well she's turned stronger heads I daresay.'

'Including yours?' Caroline asked.

'Not really. Perhaps, when I first met her. Not latterly. She's a good friend but I'd hate to have her for a wife. She's not my type.'

'What is your type?' She regretted the question at once.

'You,' he responded promptly.

'I might have known you'd say that.'

'It's true,' he assured her. 'You'll see. On our golden wedding day you'll be telling all the neighbours how we never had a cross word.'

'That's a likely tale,' she laughed.

'Perhaps a modicum of mild asperity now and then. Just to assert your authority,' he suggested. 'Not a really cross word. Why should you be cross with someone who thinks that the sun, moon and stars pale into insignificance beside you?'

'You've been reading some women's magazine.'

'Nonsense.' He laughed again. 'You

might as well give up Caroline. You haven't a chance. If you hand Richard his marching orders right away he will probably be so preoccupied with his photographic studio and Lisette that he will survive the terrible shock. It's kinder to do it quickly.'

'There's a little snag. I don't want to get married, not yet.'

'Of course not. Christmas I thought. That's always seemed to me a good time to get married. I've never understood the fashion for June weddings. Marry at Christmas and then two months of ski-ing for a honeymoon.'

'And spend it in bed with a broken leg or arm? No thanks.'

'I'm glad you agree we're getting married even if you disagree with the honeymoon plans.'

'I did no such thing.'

'Yes you did. Why argue about ski-ing if you aren't going on a honeymoon anyway?'

'I'm merely pointing out to you how impractical your ideas are. It's time someone took you down a peg or two.'

'Am I big headed?' he asked frankly.

'Not that I've noticed but you may change at any time. You've had a lot of good ideas recently.'

'The best one is marrying you.'

'I'm engaged.' She did not even say it convincingly, and he took her and kissed her. He kissed her several times.

'That's enough,' she said firmly, pushing him away. 'I have things to do.'

'Better than this?' he demanded.

'Don't fish for compliments.'

She left the room quickly before he could stop her, her heart pounding. Magnus stood where he was, thinking about her. Then he walked to the window and looked outside. He was fairly sure she wouldn't marry Richard. It was a ridiculous idea. The point was, would she marry him? He was a bit short on prospects and he didn't really know how much material possessions mattered to her. It was all very well him throwing up a promising job just like that. He knew he wouldn't starve, and having fun was more important to him than having gilt-edged prospects. Besides there really *was* a small store in Putney, Vermont, and if it wasn't big business, it was sufficient. He didn't want to run the store, but it was a form of insurance.

Caroline on the other hand was not only an undeniable aristocrat but she and her delightful father were making a lot of money out of Portcullis, and if saving was difficult, they at least lived in a manner that took some beating. The way things were going, unless there was a revolution and all the English peers were carted off in tumbrils on a one-way journey, the Eaton family had made it.

He sighed. He hoped it was all right, and he even thought it was — but she might consider him brash, cheeky and pretty much of no-account. In which case his cheerful protestations of adoration would assume a comic-opera aspect which did not amuse him.

He was struggling with these pangs of unrequited love when there was a knock and the door opened.

He looked up and saw Lisette.

8

'All alone Magnus?' Lisette asked, closing the door behind her.

'Yes. I was thinking of going into the library and doing a little work before supper time. Oh of course, you've come for your bag. Where's Richard?'

He picked up the handbag and held it out.

'At home. I borrowed his car and came over for the bag.'

'Where's your own car?'

'Richard likes driving me about.'

'I'll bet he does.' Magnus smiled. 'When I suggested you help him I didn't realise I was setting your foot on the bottom rung of a new career.'

'Bottom rung be damned,' Lisette countered with a little smile. 'I believe in starting as near the top as possible.'

'Meaning?'

'I rather think Richard is engaged to

two of us at once. What he said was that he wants to marry me and that he will sort out the mess with Caroline.'

'Oh. It's gone that far has it?'

'Yes. Pleased?'

'Um.' He tried to look unconcerned but she was mocking him with her laughter.

'That's what you wanted all the time. You picked on me to help Richard because you hoped I'd complicate things with Caroline and leave the coast clear for you.'

'I may have had certain dreams.'

'You're a cunning man, Magnus Manisty.'

'If you want Richard and you're getting him, I can't see what you're complaining about,' he objected.

'I'm not complaining and neither are you. I think it's working out rather well. Of course just how long it will take Richard to pluck up courage and break his engagement is another matter. I shall have to keep egging him on.'

'I'm sure you will.'

'You know, we do understand one another,' she told him. 'You can kiss me — for old time's sake.'

'With pleasure.'

He took her in his arms and kissed her. After a second she grumbled. 'Make it a proper one. You used to do better than that. It's your last chance.'

She pulled his face to hers and Caroline, opening the door silently, recoiled from the sight. She stared for what seemed like an hour but was a matter of a few seconds. It was long enough to establish (a) that they were kissing, (b) that it was no friendly peck but the real thing and (c) that they seemed to be enjoying it enormously.

She closed the door and leaned against it, her head reeling. The snake, she thought. He wanted to marry her and he was busy devouring his ex-girl-friend. He was a Bluebeard, a potential multiple-bigamist, a double-crossing double-talking rat. Shaken she went into the kitchen where she brewed the strongest cup of tea she had had for a long time.

Meantime Magnus was carefully removing Lisette's lipstick from his mouth.

'That will give you something to remember me by,' Lisette told him lightly.

'As if I needed anything. I think I did Richard a better turn than I intended. Well, thanks for telling me the good news Lisette. I shall be on hand to console Caroline when he breaks it to her.'

'I won't wait. I only came for my handbag and Richard is developing a film. He's waiting for me. In the dark room.'

'Har.' Magnus winked vulgarly and held open the door for her.

'Goodbye Magnus. See you at the wedding.'

'Certainly, if you invite me. You wouldn't like me to give you away, would you?'

'That might not be wise.' She

laughed and walked away, and he closed the door absently.

So, at last the coast was clear, or practically clear. Richard was securely trapped by Lisette and Caroline was no longer otherwise committed. He executed a little dance step in his exuberance and then went off to consult one or two books in the library. It was the maid who disturbed him.

'Supper's ready Mr. Manisty.'

'Thanks, I'll be right along.'

He closed the book he had been browsing through, replaced it on the shelf, straightened his jumper, and left the room. Caroline and Vivian were sitting out on the patio and he took the vacant chair.

'How are things?' Vivian asked.

'Fine, fine. I've got more time to spare now so I'm going ahead quickly. Oh, Caroline, Lisette came back for her handbag. I gave it to her.'

'Yes, I know.'

'You know? Oh did you meet her on the way out?'

Caroline gave a sinister little chuckle. 'Not quite. On the way, perhaps; but not out, judging by what I saw.'

'Huh?'

'Nothing.'

'Oh.' He looked at her curiously. She was giving him a steely stare which astonished him. He could not think what he had done to merit it. Luckily Vivian was in a chatty frame of mind and he and Magnus kept the conversation going while Caroline ate in studied silence.

As soon as they had finished the meal she excused herself and went into the hall to use the telephone there. She dialled the number of Verney Hall and demanded to speak to Richard. After a pause he came on the line.

'Yes? Verney here.'

'About time Richard. This is Caroline.'

'Oh, why didn't the silly girl say so.'

'I didn't tell her. Is that Taylor woman with you?'

'Lisette? As a matter of fact she is.

We're looking at some film of her I shot today.'

'Richard, do I have to remind you that we are engaged?'

'No. That is . . . no.' Her attack took him off guard. How could he bring up the subject of Lisette and himself, he wondered.

'I'm glad to hear it. I don't suppose it has occurred to you that your behaviour is dishonourable . . . '

'I say.'

'But it is, Richard. People will start talking if indeed they haven't already started. I think you should pay more attention to me. I know you take a few photographs each week and that they have to be enlarged and nicely printed. That is no reason why you shouldn't come here to see me every day, now that you've given up your job in the bank. You only live three and a half miles away, door to door.'

'Yes. Well, I suppose I've been a bit preoccupied.'

'I understand,' she interrupted smoothly.

'I'm just suggesting that as of this moment you begin to treat me as what I am — the girl you are going to marry. I particularly want you to come tomorrow. We must settle the wedding date.'

'Wedding date?' he asked in a strangulated voice.

'Yes dearest. We don't want to wait too long, do we?'

'Oh . . . er . . . oh no. Of course not. What?' He was gibbering, bewildered.

'So we must settle it. When will you come?'

'Ummm . . . um . . . '

'Come after breakfast. I'm sure you don't have any work to do. It's Sunday.'

'Well, I have some photographs . . . '

'You could do them for an hour or two in the evening. Oh, and Richard . . . '

'Yes?' he asked warily.

'Miss Taylor. I don't think you need to see her again, do you? I mean, she has served her purpose, hasn't she? Let her go back to earning her grubby little living, there's a darling.'

'I can't just drop her . . .'

'Of course you can. Would you like me to speak to her?' Caroline asked sweetly.

'No, no, please don't.'

'I'm sure you'll handle everything beautifully. Love me?'

'Pardon?'

'I asked if you love me.' Caroline spoke with deliberation.

'Yes, yes. Love you. Yes, yes.'

'Then don't forget it darling.'

She hung up and left him, nerveless and limp with barely enough strength to replace the receiver. Caroline returned to the sitting-room to her coffee.

'Who were you calling?' Vivian asked.

'Richard. He hasn't been very attentive recently. I was just making sure he'd come here to see me tomorrow.'

'Oh,' Vivian said, losing interest, while Magnus frowned.

'Yes. We must fix the date for the wedding. I thought we might get married at Christmas. It would be nice don't you think? I can't understand the modern predilection for June weddings, can you?'

'What! No, not really. I suppose Christmas is a good time,' Vivian admitted half-heartedly, and Magnus gaped to hear himself quoted so shamelessly.

'So I'm going to arrange things for December.'

'Where will you go for a honeymoon?' Vivian asked. 'The West Indies?'

'I think Austria would be nice. All that beautiful white snow, lovely little villages, it would be such a change from the usual run of honeymoons.'

'Yes.' Vivian wondered what had got into her.

'So if you'll excuse me,' she said rising, 'I think I'll have an early bath tonight and get a good night's sleep. I want to look my best for Richard tomorrow. He's coming early . . . and alone.'

'I'll walk along the corridor with you,' Magnus said quickly, getting up. 'I wanted to ask you something.'

'Make it snappy, won't you?' Caroline told him icily.

They left the room and he grabbed her arm.

'What's the idea?' he hissed. 'What's all this about you and Richard having a honeymoon in Austria? You're not marrying Richard, you're marrying me.'

'I wouldn't marry you if my life depended on it. You revolt me.'

'What?' He took a step back but held her arm.

'Let me go you big bully.'

'Caroline I demand an explanation.'

'Because my fiance is coming to discuss wedding plans? Who do you think you are, Mr. Manisty? You may be helping my father but you're not running my life. Let go.'

She shook her arm but he held on desperately.

'Caroline, what's got into you? I thought we were at least friends. When I kissed you, you didn't mind too much.'

'You snake.'

'What?'

She managed to shake free and turned to him, scarlet with indignation. 'You just leave me alone, Magnus Manisty. I can't order you to stay away from Portcullis, not when you're involved with my father, but you stay away from me, do you hear? For if you don't I'm going to make you look damned stupid. *I don't like you*. I don't want to see you again. Is that clear enough for you, you conceited Yank?'

His jaw dropped before her quiet fury and she turned and walked off leaving him entirely baffled. The truth did not occur to him for, so far as he knew, he and Lisette had been alone in a room behind closed doors. So he looked for an explanation elsewhere and could not find one.

He went back into the room.

'Funny,' Vivian said looking up with pleasure. 'She hasn't mentioned her wedding at all, and now suddenly it's important. I've never understood the opposite sex. You know, if the Almighty really did invent the whole system, why didn't he do it more sensibly? If it had been all men and we'd been able to lay eggs all by ourselves, it would have been much more satisfactory.'

'Definitely.'

'You never met Caroline's mother. Wonderful woman and a real beauty, but just like Caroline. You never knew when she'd do something completely unexpected. I rather thought Caroline was getting over Richard Verney, but it seems I was wrong.'

'We both were,' Magnus assured him.

'You thought so too did you? How strange. It only goes to show.' The earl heaved a sigh. 'Now, what were you telling me earlier about displaying postcards?'

Magnus tried to concentrate on the matter in hand.

★   ★   ★

A week later Magnus was busy moving into his new cottage one evening, very fed up with the cold treatment Caroline was handing out and the fact that whenever he went to the manor he seemed to bump into a silent Richard, when a familiar little VW drew up. He put down a hammer he was using and went to the open door. Lisette walked up the paved path towards him, her look as black at the polo-necked sweater she was wearing.

'Hullo,' he said dully.

'Hullo yourself.'

'Oh, what's wrong with you?'

'What do you think? Do you know what's going on between Caroline and Richard?'

'A wedding.'

'What's been happening, Magnus?'

'Come and sit down and have a drink. Gin?'

'Vodka. A double, with ginger ale.'

'Coming up. I don't know what's going on. I was beginning to think everything was fine when suddenly she told me I was a snake in the grass and then began to invite Richard round at all hours. Why he doesn't move in, I

can't think. It would save them both
time.'

'What have you been doing?'

'Me? I've been banging my head on
the wall. Don't ask me about it. I
thought *you* had it all settled with
Richard.'

'I had, and then the little worm
suddenly began to make excuses not to
see me. He telephoned me to say he
had a sore throat, that he had to go to
Cowes of all unlikely places, that he was
too busy — you name anything stupid,
he tried it. Then I found he's been
haunting Caroline Eaton, *your* friend.'

'Why is it,' Magnus grumbled, 'that
whenever anyone doesn't like someone
else, they always decide that they're *my*
friend.'

'I thought she was your friend.'

'And Richard was yours. Look
Lisette, something has misfired, but
stop pointing your finger at me. I know
no more than you do. Caroline won't
even talk to me. I'm not going back
there for a long time. I've got work to

do here, and I can telephone her father if I want to talk to him.'

'You're sure you didn't back out, and turn her loose on Richard again?'

'Back out?' His face gave her the answer. 'I love her dammit. I want to marry her.'

Lisette drank half the vodka at a gulp.

'Then we don't know what's wrong. Well I'm not giving Richard up.'

'It's easier for you. He has to be polite. She doesn't have to be polite to me.'

'What will you do?'

'I'll tell you what I'm going to do,' Magnus said suddenly making up his mind. 'I've got to finish moving into this cottage, which will take another two days. Then I've got to finish that book, which will take another two weeks at the outside. After that I'm going back to Putney, Vermont, to see my mother and father and look up a few old friends. I shall have a holiday at home for a couple of months. Then I'll come back here, attend to the final arrangements about the book, and I'm off to Austria for the winter. I'm fed up with women.'

'Running away?' she asked, surprised at the news.

'Call it that if it makes you feel better. I know when I'm not wanted. I'm overdue for a visit to my folks anyway. I might as well go as soon as I'm able.'

'I'm not giving up so easily.'

'I wish you luck. I'll give you a key to this place and you can use it while I'm away if you want.'

'Why should I want?'

'I don't know. It will be standing here empty anyway. If you manage to get Richard away from Caroline, you can have a love nest.'

'Listen Magnus,' she exclaimed ignoring the jibe about the love nest, 'if I do get Richard back, and I fully intend to for I really want him and she can't have him, that will leave the coast clear for you again.'

'You don't understand, Lisette. Richard is torn in two directions. He doesn't look at all happy up at Portcullis. He's ripe for the taking. It's just that he's far too weak to tell Caroline to jump in the Thames. It's not like that with Caroline. She hates the sight of me. With or without Richard, I'm bad news to her. So forget it.'

'Poor you.'

'I'll recover. Pity though.' He sighed miserably.

He stood at the door as Lisette left, and as she walked to her car Caroline drove past in hers. She glanced coldly at Lisette's familiar figure, and her lips tightened. So be it, she thought. Lisette and Magnus stared after her as she disappeared from sight, and then she waved to him and she too was off. He returned to the house to his black brooding.

Vivian Eaton was bewildered by the sudden change in things around his ancestral pile. Magnus no longer visited them, but telephoned with brief enquiries and briefer reports. True, things were going extremely well, but it looked decidedly as if Magnus were 'dropping' them. Vivian missed the young American. As for Caroline, she was in a permanent bad temper and Richard was for ever turning up and mooning about the place silently. The world had gone mad. The only consolation was that business was booming and he had taken on a salaried manager, something he had been thinking about for a year or two. The expense was justified now, and it would leave him more free time. He was keenly interested in the time museum and also in his own collection of postcards and muffs. They helped to keep his mind off what was going on around him.

Eventually Magnus turned up one Friday morning and Vivian sent for coffee.

'I've missed you,' he said bluntly.

'Well I've been busy sir. I finished work on the manuscript. I took it to a woman yesterday, who will type it and send it on to Laker & Day while I'm away.'

'Away?'

'That's why I came to see you. I've been pretty busy and I need a holiday. I'm going to visit my parents for a couple of months.'

'Aren't they in America?'

'Yes,' Magnus laughed. 'I'm an American, remember?'

'You're going for two months?'

'I'll be back in November and then in December I'm off again to Austria. It all fits in well. I'll be back again in time to settle all the final details of the book.'

'I see.'

'I've brought you a carbon of the original manuscript, but the woman who is doing the typing will send you a carbon of the properly typed thing. If anything occurs to you, don't bother about me, just ring Laker & Day and tell them. It is understood that the thing must have your approval.'

'Hey, weren't you going to do a brochure on this Charles the Second business?'

'It's done. I've got a copy with me.

You only have to read it, and when I come back we'll iron out any changes and I'll have it printed in lots of time for next year.'

'You're a fast worker.'

'I have been at it full-time, remember. How's everything?'

'We've had a record month.'

'Good.'

Caroline opened the door and stood stock still.

'You've got company, sorry.'

'What do you mean, 'company'?' Vivian asked. 'It's Magnus.'

'I'll leave you to it.'

She turned and closed the door and Vivian stared.

'She's in a funny mood these days.'

'She'll be busy about the wedding,' Magnus answered tonelessly.

'More like a funeral. Take my advice, don't get married, and if you do, don't have daughters. Mysterious creatures. You're not planning on marrying, are you?'

'I did think of it, but I changed my mind.'

'Sensible fellow,' Vivian chuckled. 'Who was it? That slinky model?'

'Lisette? Good lord no. I was never serious about her. No, someone else.'

'Ah, well, I shan't pry. Yes, quite seriously, you'd think it was a funeral they were preparing for. Caroline's bad tempered and Richard hardly opens his mouth. I can't think what they see in one another, but that's another thing you see. Sons-in-law. You can't pick your own. Damned unfair. Still you don't want to worry about trifles like that. When do you go?'

'Tomorrow.'

'So soon?'

Magnus nodded. 'Yes. I came to say goodbye for the moment. Of course I'll drop you a line from Putney, U.S.A., and I'll be contacting you as soon as I return. Laker & Day have my address in case anything comes up about the book, but I doubt it. It's turned out well.'

'What have you called it?'

Magnus opened the briefcase he had

been carrying and took out two envelopes, one rather bulkier than the other.

'Here you are. *The Laughing Buccaneer.*'

'What?'

'You'll see why when you read it. It's damned good material if you'll pardon the expression. A cross between *Captain Blood* and *Forever Amber* with a touch of the *Forsyte Saga* thrown in. I wondered if it shouldn't have been written by a professional but I think I've managed to keep it light and readable, and it's all fact. That's what's so marvellous.'

'It beats me how you make it sound interesting. I know the family history fairly well.'

'Yes, but to you it always has been just that — family history. I came to it as an outsider and saw the human interest underlying all the dry facts.'

'Well I'm looking forward to reading it.'

'I hope you aren't shocked. If you

expected something that could have been entitled 'The Eatons of Portcullis. A Family Study' you'll be disappointed.

'No, no, I'm all in favour of something lively. This is a competitive business and some of my stately home rivals have a lot to offer. I've got to fight them on contemporary lines. It sounds jolly interesting.'

'Well anyway that's it. I think it might do well, and of course it will be beautifully illustrated and everybody who reads it will be under no misapprehensions about their right to visit Portcullis three times a week for a modest fee. It ought to help whip up trade a little.'

'I honestly don't know how to thank you. You've had nothing out of all this.'

'Look at all the food and drink I've disposed of. Besides I've enjoyed it. You can give me a free pass for life.'

'You already have one, dear boy. No Eaton would ever turn you away from the gates of Portcullis.'

Magnus thought of Caroline and

smiled wryly. 'No,' he agreed hollowly.

After another fifteen minutes he took his leave. On his way out he almost bumped into Caroline in the hall. She hesitated and coloured.

'Hullo,' she greeted him.

'Hullo Caroline.'

'Business finished?' she asked brightly.

'I guess you might say that the business is finished. If you'll excuse me I have some last-minute shopping and packing to do. Goodbye Caroline. Have a nice wedding.'

He was off before she could stop him. She stood irresolute trying to make sense out of his words, and then ran to the door. He was striding along the drive towards the waiting Porsche. She frowned in perplexity and then sought out her father.

'What did Magnus want?' she asked abruptly.

'He came to let me have a copy of the book. It's finished.'

'Oh good.'

'And to say goodbye.'

'He just said goodbye to me too. Where's he going?' she asked.

'Didn't he tell you? He's off to America. Putney, Vermont, to be precise.'

Caroline stared at her father.

'Tomorrow,' Vivian added, turning to the manuscript on the sofa.

'Oh,' Caroline said in a small voice, and suddenly she felt very depressed.

9

'What?' Richard Verney asked, hardly able to believe his ears.

'I said you make me sick. I wouldn't marry you if you were the last man left alive. I'm sorry Richard but I don't want to marry you.'

'That's all right,' he said, a shade too quickly but she did not notice.

'I don't want to marry anyone. You can have your ring back.'

'No, you keep it.'

'I don't want it,' she said irritably, pulling it from her finger and holding it out. 'You have it. No hard feelings Richard, but I'm just not ready for marriage. I don't love you. I release you from your promise.'

'That's jolly decent of you,' he said, thinking of Lisette.

'You'd better go and call her hadn't you?'

'What's that?'

'Lisette. You wanted her all the time, didn't you?'

He stared at her in admiration. 'Well, yes, towards the end I did wonder if I hadn't been a bit premature, but . . . I don't mean . . . '

'Oh, stop apologising Richard. It's a very bad trait. You don't love me either. It was a sort of habit, our being paired off together.'

'Well, if you're sure,' he said eagerly.

'Quite sure. Now go away.'

He gave her the first really happy smile she had seen on his face for some time and almost ran from the room. Caroline sat down in her favourite chair and felt sorry for herself. At least she had got rid of Richard, which had had to be done. That had been easy enough.

What did the future hold? Nothing. For years everyone had assumed that she and Richard were a two-some. Then there had appeared on the scene Magnus Manisty. Now Magnus had gone and there was no two-some. She felt lonely and rejected and very fed up with life. She had been wrong about Magnus; she knew that now, for she had discovered by dint of discreet enquiry from Richard that Lisette, far from being Magnus's girl, never saw Magnus. There was nothing at all between them.

It had all been too bad, and she still didn't know why Magnus and Lisette had to make love in public if they didn't feel that way about one another; or even why Lisette visited Magnus while he was moving into that empty cottage further down the road. If it hadn't been for that torrid necking scene, which she had stumbled into, mused Caroline, she and Magnus might . . .

She stopped thinking about it. She had been wrong, obviously, and Magnus had gone. Now Richard was free to chase up Lisette and she was free to stew in her own juice. She sat brooding till supper was ready.

'You're looking extremely pensive my

dear,' Vivian commented during the meal.

'I am. I'm wondering what I've done.'

'I'm overcome by curiosity. Explain.'

'I've just sacked Richard,' she laughed. 'I gave him his marching orders. I expect he's already on the telephone to the Taylor girl to let her know the good news.'

'Like that, is it?' he asked.

'I don't know why I ever got engaged to him,' she answered.

'If you want my opinion it's good news. I like Richard enormously, as a sort of neighbour, but I didn't fancy him as my one and only son-in-law. Not enough sneddum.'

'What on earth is sneddum?' she demanded.

'It's a word I picked up. Scottish. It means a combination of guts, initiative, common sense — well, you get the general idea. I wonder why I remembered it. I haven't heard it for years. When we used to go shooting up near

Ballater, when my father was alive, we had a ghillie who used the word a lot. I thought it was expressive. Anyway Richard had none. Charming fellow no doubt, but hardly the sort who would set any girl's heart fluttering I'd have thought.'

'Quite right,' she agreed. 'Not all girls want to have their hearts set fluttering, but I'm afraid I need a more aggressive sort of mate than Richard would have been. Anyway where do I go from here?'

'Why go anywhere?' Vivian demanded. 'You're only twenty-two. There's no hurry.'

'I'll soon be twenty-three and I hardly know any men. I've been out of circulation for a long time. I'll end up like Aunt Selina.'

'You mustn't do that. What would happen to Portcullis if you did? The title dies with me, but I don't want to see the house go to the National Trust, or worse still, to strangers. You must get about more.'

'Just what I was thinking. I must

write to Rowena.'

'Who is she?'

'Don't you remember Rowena Marsden? I brought her here several times when I was at Westonbirt. She was a great chum of mine. I've rather lost touch but I can soon remedy that.'

'The one whose father had a house in Northumberland and owned an airline or something?'

'Two charter companies, darling, not an airline. That's right. They are hardly ever at home but if I write to Dwindledon Hall I'm pretty sure she'll get it.'

'You want to go up there, do you?'

'No sweetheart,' Caroline explained patiently. 'Unless Rowena has acquired religion and gone into a closed order, she will be raising hell somewhere. She always did at school. She'll have hordes of friends.'

'Sounds fun. You need a change.'

Vivian was pleased at the turn events had taken. Ideally he'd have liked Caroline to link up with Magnus

Manisty, but he was realistic enough to know that ideal situations rarely prevail. At least she had got rid of Richard and if she re-established contact with old friends some suitable man might turn up in due course, someone he personally would feel happy about. It occurred to him that having a daughter was a bit of a responsibility. He hadn't thought of Caroline in that way for some years, but it was true. He'd be glad to see her safely settled. But, he wondered, what was 'safely settled' nowadays? It was a difficult question to answer.

Things were going well at Portcullis. The season was past its peak but visitors still poured in three days a week spending like mad, sales were soaring, and much more important all the plans for the future were maturing nicely. He was really looking forward to the end of the season when he would be able to devote more time to the time museum. As it was, the Eaton Collection of postcards, ladies' muffs and bric-à-brac was taking shape nicely.

More to the point, Laker & Day were ecstatic about Magnus's book, *The Laughing Buccaneer* and Vivian himself thought it was a splendid piece of work. It did indeed read more like *Captain Blood* than serious family history, yet Magnus had been careful not to over-embroider the true facts. The book was confidently expected to sell widely. Some minor revision of two chapters was needed and Magnus would be back soon to take care of that.

That afternoon's post brought a short letter from Magnus, at home in Vermont, giving the date of his return. Vivian read it with satisfaction. It would be good to see the young American again, to have a chat about progress. It was extraordinary how Magnus had come into their lives, what an impact he had had. Then he realised that on the reverse of the last page there was a postscript. He read it with mild surprise.

'You may wonder what I have been doing with myself all these weeks. I've been working in the afternoons most days — writing a book. It seemed a pity to let all that expert knowledge go to waste so I've written a novel about an American who inherits a stately home. I haven't cribbed very much, and it is set in Cheshire where I once spent a holiday. I sent it off to a firm of publishers over here this morning, and am already wondering what to do next, so I won't be sorry to come back to Britain for a few weeks to tie up loose ends. I've called my novel *The Ermine Touch*, which seemed to combine being cryptic with the vague suggestion of aristocracy, and doesn't give away too much. Anyway that is what I thought at the time. I'm pretty awful at titles. Of course nobody will know I wrote your book, as I promised your daughter some time ago that I would put her name on it. After all, she is to get the proceeds to help stave off the encroachment of bureaucratic thieves.'

Vivian went off in search of Caroline and found her in the rose garden.

'Ah there you are. I've had a letter from Magnus.'

'Oh?'

'Caroline, did you know that he was writing that book under your name?'

'No. Oh wait, yes, he did say something once but I shouldn't think he meant it. He said that as he didn't want the proceeds from the book, he might as well put it in my name since I was the one who would need the money. I didn't take it particularly seriously. After all, he wrote it. The money is neither here nor there but he won't want somebody else's name on the cover.'

'He says in his letter that nobody will know who wrote it because he promised to put your name on it.'

'Writing about me, was he?' she asked, suddenly looking interested.

'No.' Her face fell but Vivian did not notice. 'He was writing about the fact that he has written a novel while he's in America. About stately homes. He just mentioned in passing that his name wouldn't be on *The Laughing Bucca-neer*.'

'I don't want my name on it,' she told him in a grouchy voice.

'Somebody's name will have to go on it He'll be here in a few days so I can discuss it with him then. What's your objection?'

'I didn't write it and I don't want it to look as though I'm pretending I did. He did it all by himself. Let him take the credit if there is any.'

'There will be plenty of that. It's going to sell well, they say.'

'Fine. It's nothing to do with me.'

'Aren't you even interested?' he asked her.

'Not particularly.'

He shrugged and turned away. She was in one of her moods again.

★   ★   ★

Magnus paid off the taxi and walked up the drive to the cottage, carrying his two light-weight suitcases. He opened the door and saw several envelopes behind it. When he had put down the cases he picked them up. Four were circulars, one was a receipt for a bill he had paid before going to Vermont, and the other was private. He slit open the envelope with his thumb and took out two folded sheets of heavy paper. He recognised Lisette's handwriting, and taped to the paper was the key to the door. He detached it and slipped it into his pocket.

The letter was exuberant. Richard had broken it off with Caroline and come back to her and they were now officially engaged. She had not needed the key but she had come in and dusted and tidied in his absence and hoped that she had left everything the way he wanted it.

He put it on a side table and glanced around as he took in what she had written. Richard and Caroline were through. How on earth had Richard got up enough courage to break free? Not that it mattered. Caroline loathed him,

Magnus, and had said so in no uncertain fashion. He grunted quietly and took his cases upstairs.

By the time he had picked up the Porsche from the garage looking after it, done essential shopping and taken it all home, it was time for some sort of evening meal. He changed into more comfortable clothes and went out to an unpretentious restaurant. Tomorrow he would have to do something about his own plans, which he had ditched. He no longer wanted a restaurant in Walton, but he was committed to buying the premises. Well, he reflected, it ought not to be too difficult to get rid of them, but it would all have to be tidied up and the loose ends dealt with.

He did not intend to go to Portcullis that night, but temptation was strong, and after driving as far as the gates, he went home and telephoned. His call was answered by Vivian.

'Magnus here.'

'My dear chap, how good to hear your voice again. You at the cottage?'

'Yes, I got in earlier today. How are you?'

'Splendid. Splendid. Come round and have coffee or something.'

'Isn't it a bit late? I don't want to disturb Caroline and you.'

'Caroline is not here and Selina is up in her room. I'm wide open to being disturbed.'

'In that case I'll come round.'

Magnus hung up and wondered where Caroline was. He drove to Portcullis where Vivian greeted him joyously. When they were seated comfortably Magnus asked, 'Where's your daughter?'

'Oh Caroline went off five days ago. She's in Kenya.'

'What in heaven's name is she doing there?'

'On safari, gazing at wild animals. She broke it up with Richard Verney, you know, and became very broody. In the end I persuaded her to take a thousand pounds out of the bank and go away and not come back till it was spent.'

'She's alone in Kenya?' Magnus demanded.

'Lord no. She's taken up with some old school chum who has got a party together — about ten of them I think.'

'I see, I see. It must make things quiet for you.'

'Confidentially I don't mind that. I've got so many interests. You've seen the revisions to the book of course. Any problems?'

'No. I can attend to them inside a fortnight quite easily. When does Caroline come back?'

If Vivian wondered why Magnus sometimes referred to her as 'Caroline' and other times as 'your daughter', he did not display the fact.

'I don't know. Before Christmas anyway. They don't seem to have any fixed plans. There's talk of going somewhere for some game fishing.'

'Really having fun. She must have been very glad to get rid of Richard, by the sound of it.'

'Not so glad as I was. He's got

himself engaged to that girl you introduced to us. Lisette. It was in *The Times*.'

'I heard about it.'

'Everything ends satisfactorily,' Vivian laughed. 'Yes, well, more coffee?'

'Thank you.'

Vivian poured and talked. 'We're closed after this week and I can get down to business. There are a lot of points I'd like to consult you about. Not very important perhaps, but I value your judgement.'

'Count on me.'

'I don't want to make a nuisance of myself.'

'Honestly sir, I'm at a bit of a loose end. I'll do the revisions and alterations in the afternoons after lunch. It's simple enough. That leaves me free the rest of the time.'

'Then come here as often as you can in the mornings. Selina will be delighted to see you again. How is your own book going?'

'I haven't heard anything.'

'Oh. Now what is this about using Caroline's name on the *Buccaneer*?'

'That's what I intend.'

'She's not keen. Doesn't like to appear a fraud. After all, as she says, you wrote it.'

'True.' She would not want her name on his despised work, would she he thought? Of course not. She loathed him. 'It was a gesture. I haven't signed the contract with Laker & Day yet but I'll see the money from the book is all paid to you. There's the question of copies for sale here. We'll have to thrash out terms with them about that bit of it. Perhaps we both ought to go up to London one day.'

'Splendid idea.'

'Shall I ring them tomorrow and lay on something? For, say, the end of next week? Thursday or Friday?'

'Make it Thursday week, if you can. If not, I'll fit in with whatever it is. Good idea.'

Magnus stayed quite late, yarning. When he finally returned to his cottage he thought of Caroline. Her face was always before him, and he had missed her terribly. He loved her more than ever which was not only ridiculous, it was stupid, for there was most definitely no hope in that quarter. Why did it take so long to get over her? No other female had ever had quite this effect on him. He tried to picture her in Kenya. He wondered what sort of party it was. Were there virile young men in bush jackets and hats with snakeskin bands, looking like youthful film stars, playing the part of the Big White Hunter Bwana? He felt ridiculously jealous. He hadn't liked to ask too many questions of Vivian, so his imagination ran riot. Perhaps there were a lot of men and only two or three girls. She would have forgotten all about him.

He turned and kicked the door savagely, stubbing his toe for he was wearing corduroy sneakers. He hopped up and down, swearing silently, and then had a very hot bath, a cup of chocolate, and went to bed where he slept very badly.

For the next two weeks he worked fairly hard. He went to the manor almost every morning, after he had done his simple household chores and his shopping. In the afternoons he put the finishing touches to the manuscript of *The Laughing Buccaneer* and the evenings were spent attending to various bits of business. In the end he decided that he would go ahead with his plans for a restaurant. Once it was open it would provide him with an income. It was an investment, and even if he himself didn't stay in Walton, and he had no intention of remaining on Caroline's doorstep and torturing himself, it was no reason why he shouldn't go ahead with the original scheme.

At the end of two weeks he heard from the New York publishers. They had read *The Ermine Touch*, liked it and wanted to publish it. They proposed an advance of ten thousand dollars against royalties. He studied the document delightedly and wrote his acceptance. Apart from the fact that the money might be very useful, for he was going to tie up almost all his capital in this restaurant, he hated to think of all that work going to waste. One question however haunted him. What were his plans for the next book, they demanded? The answer was that he had none. It was something he would have to do something about.

Suddenly things slackened off. There was nothing immediate he could do about his restaurant, nothing urgent to do in any other respect, and even Vivian Eaton had no need to consult him any further although he always made him very welcome. Magnus decided it was time to be off. It was a little early yet for skiing but if he went to Austria now he could put in a few weeks' work, planning a second novel, mapping out the course of the action, and enjoying the Austrian scenery and food. He booked into the hotel in Oberwald where he had spent his first European winter-sports holiday. It would be something of a sentimental journey, his first time back.

When he went to take his leave of Vivian and Selina they were once again sorry to see him go.

'When will you be back?' Vivian demanded.

'I don't know. Before Easter. I've got to get my things out of the cottage by then. They won't let me have it any longer.'

'Where will you go after that?' Selina asked.

'Who knows. Perhaps back to Vermont.'

'Why not stay here for a bit?' Vivian asked.

Magnus smiled politely. He did not want to hurt Vivian's feelings but nothing on earth would get him under the same roof as Caroline, not after that last scene. He was flesh and blood, after all, and very much in love with her.

'We'll see,' he replied. 'You've got my address if anything crops up, but I don't expect it will, and of course I'll be in

241

touch with you too, so that takes care of everything.'

'Caroline will be so sorry she missed you,' Selina said with a sigh. 'It's such a pity you can't stay longer.'

'I expect Caroline has forgotten me by now,' Magnus said bravely.

'Oh no. She wouldn't do that.'

He did not contradict her. He said goodbye and drove off. Vivian turned to his sister.

'Always coming and going. I wish he'd stay put.'

'There's nothing to hold him. Now if Caroline had been at home . . . '

'You don't think he's interested in her, do you?' Vivian asked keenly.

'He may be. She's certainly interested in him.'

'Are you sure? I had a distinct impression that she didn't care for him much. Some of the things she said . . . '

'My dear Vivian, when will you learn that what a girl says and what she means are two entirely different things.'

'I don't suppose I ever shall, now.'

'You wait till Easter when he comes back. You must make certain Caroline hasn't gone off again when that happens.'

'I shouldn't think so,' her brother laughed. 'Her money won't last that long.'

'What on earth has money to do with it?' Selina demanded. 'When we let her know he is coming back, she'll stay. You'll see.'

'I told her he was here and it didn't bring her home.'

'How can she come back in the middle of the trip?' Selina demanded. 'Be reasonable.'

Vivian looked at her perplexed.

'You really do think there is something between them?'

'Oh yes,' she said airily. 'They may not know it, but it's plain enough.'

'What sort of answer is that?' he grumbled, thinking again that women were indeed mysterious, even sisters.

10

Caroline was very brown. She sat in a white bikini, drinking a long cold drink, her hair gleaming like silver, so bleached was it. Jackie Groves, himself tanned the colour of old leather, and lean and tough as whipcord, thought she was the loveliest girl he had ever seen. He had come out to Kenya as Rowena's current boyfriend, but he felt less and less inclined towards the admittedly luscious, dark-haired Rowena. Caroline, who was remarkably unaware of the tumultuous feelings she aroused in her friend's escort, smiled at him.

'Isn't it lovely here by the ocean?' she asked.

They had come to Malindi, on the coast, after a prolonged safari which took them into Serengeti in the neighbouring Tanzania. It had been new and exciting and there was a real pleasure in relaxing round a camp fire at night after an exhausting day. Better still were the nights in game lodges with hot baths, big wood-burning fire-places and proper dining-rooms.

Caroline had learned not to think very much about Magnus Manisty and how she had botched things there. There were, after all, as she kept reminding herself assiduously, many other pebbles on the beach. Indeed she thoroughly enjoyed being in Rowena's safari party and meeting a whole lot of other young people of her own age. Now, after the arduous days in the bush, they had come to the coast to relax and have fun. There was talk of going on a fishing expedition to some place called Mafia Island, to the south, but Caroline had not decided about this. In the first place the timetable had gone wrong and they had spent much longer in Tanzania than they had anticipated, and also more time in the Kenya game reserves, and secondly she was not very interested in fishing. She was considering going home fairly soon.

'Very lovely,' Jackie said in reply to her remark about the beach scene. 'You improve it.'

'Thank you kind sir.' She spoke lightly but the compliment was not unwelcome.

'I mean it.'

'And I meant it when I said thank you. We girls need to safeguard our morale. Here's Rowena.'

Jackie looked at Rowena with a shade less enthusiasm than was seemly, but apparently she did not notice this. She pulled up a chair into the shade of the big striped beach umbrella and sat down.

'Phew, warm isn't it? I'm going in for another swim. Have you been goggling on the reef yet?'

'Early this morning,' Caroline answered.

'Gorgeous, isn't it?'

'How long are we staying here?' Caroline asked.

'I don't know. About a week or ten

days. I have to make arrangements about the fishing trip this afternoon. Why?'

'I don't think I'll come along. I'll go back to Nairobi and then home.'

'You said you weren't keen. I tell you what Caroline. The fishing should last about two weeks, and then I'm heading for Austria for some ski-ing. I'm going to a place called Oberwald. Why don't we meet there?'

'I hadn't thought of that. I can't ski.'

'You can learn quickly enough. It's fun. Besides you water ski, don't you?'

'Yes.'

'You shouldn't have too much trouble. It isn't exactly the same thing but at least you can keep your balance. Think about it.'

Caroline was already thinking about it. It was all right for Rowena whose father was weighted down with money. Rowena spent most of her life on holiday, chasing from one adventure to another. She was an only child and outrageously spoiled.

'I'll see.'

'You'd enjoy it.'

What Rowena did not know was that Caroline had just heard from her Aunt Selina that Magnus Manisty had gone away again and was somewhere in Austria. Selina's intention was to make sure that Caroline would be at Portcullis next time Magnus was around, but she was achieving the opposite effect. Caroline was instead thinking that if she went to Austria with Rowena she probably couldn't afford another holiday at Easter. If, on the other hand, she went home now she could go away again before Magnus came back on the scene. That way she wouldn't have to see him at all. It was too embarrassing even to think about meeting him. Therefore she did not jump at Rowena's suggestion. There was also the remote but not completely impossible chance that she might meet Magnus in Austria. She did not think it likely. He was pretty much of an expert skier and she expected that he would have some hidden corner of the country where he could use his expertise to the full without tourists milling all round.

Rowena gave her a puzzled look. Sometimes Caroline was great fun, the life and soul of the party, and at other times she went all moody and withdrew into herself. She would have to talk to her about it.

'Coming for a swim then?' she asked.

'I'm going to goggle on the reef again,' Caroline answered, picking up mask and flippers.

'You can keep me company Jackie,' Rowena told that young man. 'Come along.'

He took one last look at Caroline, and obediently followed. Caroline was slower, and set off at a tangent. She wanted to be alone, partly because goggling is not a particularly social activity, and partly because she really wanted to think. She was not quite ready yet to go back to Walton. She was still enjoying her freedom. A vague idea began to form in her mind.

That evening early, while she was in her bath, Rowena came into her room looking for her.

'Where are you Caroline?'

'In the bath.'

'Oh.' Rowena opened the door and closed it again. 'Hullo. That looks nice. Listen, a few of us are going dancing tonight at a little place called the Tropicana. You coming?'

'Yes, all right.'

'There are just three of us, so you will make up a fourth. Jackie and Tom, you and me. The rest are all too whacked and Linda has succeeded in getting too much sun after all this time.'

'I'd like to come.'

'I knew you would. What about Oberwald in three weeks' time?'

'I'll let you know.'

'It would be nice if you would come. We'll have a super party at Christmas and the New Year.'

'Are all the others going?'

'No, just me. I've got other friends who'll be there.'

'Not even Jackie?' Caroline asked laughingly.

'He's getting Christmas off. In fact he goes up to Scotland where he visits a grandmother or something, and has a good time on his own at Aviemore. I don't mind. I believe in a change.'

'So it would be just the two of us?'

'Not exactly. There will be a whole gang. You'll like them.'

'I'll tell you before you go off to Mafia for your game fishing.'

She found the night-club rather boring and the music was too loud. Tom Ballard did his best to amuse her but she was unresponsive. Then when she was dancing with Jackie, she became aware of the fact that he was holding her tightly. She wondered if it was her imagination until she felt his fingers dig into her waist.

'You look lovely tonight, Caroline.'

'You're in a very complimentary mood today, Jackie.'

His reply was to pull her closer and she resisted this.

'What's the matter?' he murmured in her ear. 'Don't you like me?'

'Don't ask personal questions.' She kept her tone light, but he really was up to all sorts of little tricks. Nobody watching would notice, but she was aware of the pressure of his hands and arms and his attempt to draw her very close.

'This isn't a smooch,' she said, avoiding his eyes.

'We could make it one. What's the matter with you Caroline? Why are you so frigid?'

'How do you know what I am?' she chuckled. Keep it light, she thought. This is a party. He'll give up eventually.

'You know very well what I mean. Listen, I think I'll skip that fishing trip too. Why don't we go off together? Come up to Scotland with me.'

'What would your grannie say?' she teased.

'She won't know. We'll stay at a hotel.'

'More to the point,' Caroline continued, 'what would Rowena say? She's my friend, remember?'

'All's fair in love and war.'

'Which is this? War?'

'You're prickly aren't you?' he grumbled mildly.

'If you don't stop pulling at me, and making me push against your arm I shall stand on your instep Jackie, and it will hurt.'

The pressure at once slackened.

'You're not much fun are you?'

'If you want fun, have it with Rowena. You're supposed to be with her.'

'She doesn't own me, you know.'

'Nor do I. Now behave yourself.'

He gave her a dark look and began to dance woodenly. Caroline sighed inwardly. She ought to be pleased, but she wasn't. Jackie wasn't the type of man she admired at all, despite his toughness and his fantastic fitness. He was what she classed as a 'smooth operator', and she wouldn't trust him an inch. She wondered what Rowena saw in him.

She was relieved when the dance was over and they returned to the table. Rowena and Tom came up behind them and they ordered more drinks. Caroline wished it were time to go back to their hotel. It was late when they left because Rowena's stamina and zest for life were apparently inexhaustible, and she kept Jackie dancing while Tom and Caroline were content to sit and watch most of the time.

No more night-clubs, thought Caroline as she undressed and had another warm bath to take the stiffness out of her limbs. She was very tired. That wasn't what she had come along for. She would be too tired to enjoy the morning properly, unless she slept late and she didn't want to do that and miss all the fun of the beach. She towelled herself, put on a light shortie nightie, and sat down to brush her hair. Suddenly her heart leaped as reflected in the mirror, she saw her door handle turning, first one way and then the other. Had she locked it, she wondered frantically?

'Who is it?' she demanded in a loud whisper.

'Let me in.'

Not an African, but who? It was hard to tell.

'What do you want?'

'To talk to you. Open up Caroline.'

She undid the dock and opened the door a fraction. It was promptly pushed back and Jackie slipped inside.

'What do you want to lock your door for?' he demanded.

'I always do.'

'In hotels?' He sounded hurt. 'My,' he changed the subject and stood back and admired her. 'That's a sight.'

'Not for you.' She took her summer dressing-gown from the bed and slipped into it. 'What on earth do you want?'

'You of course.'

He was advancing and she backed away, alarmed. Was he serious? Apparently he was. She dodged round the other side of the bed. 'Go away you idiot.'

'Oh come on Caroline. I've had enough of Rowena.'

'I've had enough of you,' she snapped. 'Get out of here.'

He surprised her by vaulting across the bed quite easily and taking her in his arms. He began to kiss her but she turned her head away from him.

'Loosen up, will you?' he demanded.

'Jackie, even if I liked you, I wouldn't want you in my bedroom. Now will you go?'

'Of course you like me. Come on, Caroline. Relax.'

He pulled her struggling on to the bed and in anger she slapped his face. He let go and leaned back, leaving her free to slap him again, much harder.

'What the hell . . . '

'I said go.'

'For heaven's sake,' he exploded. 'I'm not raping you, am I?'

'Who can tell what you have in mind. You shouldn't be in my bedroom.'

'God, how mid-Victorian can you get?'

'I can get *early*-Victorian,' she snapped back. 'Now get out of here and don't come back. If you're very good I shan't tell Rowena.'

'I might have guessed it. You'd tell. What a little girl you are.'

She flushed at this jibe. 'Just go Jackie. I'm tired and you don't interest me.'

'All right. All right.' He got up and gave her a disgusted look. 'Ruddy Puritan.'

'I can't be bothered arguing. Out.'

He left and she locked the door. A moment later the handle turned again, and this was followed by knocking. Her mouth tightened. She switched off the overhead light, got into bed, turned off the bedside light, and pulled the sheet up over her ears. Wretched man, she thought angrily.

★   ★   ★

It was not the sunlight streaming into the room which wakened her, but the rattling of the door handle. Sleepily she pushed aside the sheet and got out, padded to the door, and opened it a fraction. She saw Rowena, in short shorts and a sun-top, and opened the door wider.

'Oh hullo. You're early.'

'I set my alarm.' Rowena's tone was not very friendly. 'What's going on?'

'What?' Caroline stared at her friend. 'I don't know. What are you talking about?'

'What was Jackie doing in here last night? I saw him leaving. I knocked but you didn't answer.'

'That was you, was it? I'd had enough for one night.'

'How charming,' Rowena said sarcastically. 'I'm glad to hear it.'

'Stop being bitchy Rowena.'

'Bitchy? My man, in your room, at two in the morning. Or more precise, coming out of it, his hair standing on end, not even answering when I tried to attract his attention. Sorry I mentioned it dearie.'

'Look, Jackie came in here all amorous. Maybe he'd had too much to drink. I had a tussle with him and persuaded him to leave. I heard you knocking but I thought it was him again; and I told you — I'd had all I could take for one night. I was tired. That's *all*.'

'How do I know you're telling the truth?' Rowena asked suspiciously.

Normally Caroline would have made allowances for her friend's agitation. She was a friendly, sympathetic person, but this morning she was irritated and tired.

'If that's what you think Rowena, you can get out too.'

'Don't take that tone with me.' Rowena was startled by Caroline's aggressiveness.

'Get out of my room. You, Jackie, all your friendly neighbourhood invaders, everyone. Just get out and leave me alone, will you?'

'If you want to be like that about it . . .'

'I told you what happened. If you don't want to believe it, go somewhere else.'

'Well, I'm glad you're not coming on the fishing trip.'

'I'm not coming anywhere. I'm leaving for Nairobi today. This is too much.'

'Good riddance.'

'At least we agree about that,' Caroline snapped back.

When Rowena had gone she went to the mirror and stared at herself. Everything was being spoiled. Damn Jackie Groves and his amorous goings-on. She'd have to make it up with Rowena, she supposed. She went and had a shower, and put on a linen dress. In the reception office she said she wanted to go back to Nairobi that day, and asked them to book her into the Norfolk Hotel and arrange transport. When she had taken care of the details and they were making up her bill, she went into breakfast. Rowena came and joined her at the table where she chose to sit alone.

'Darling I'm sorry. I've been talking to Jackie. It was just that . . . well, you *are* attractive and you know what men are.'

'I'm learning. Forget it Rowena. I woke up on the wrong side.'

'You won't leave then?'

'I will, if you don't mind. I ought to get back anyway.'

'Not because of this, Caroline. I thought we were friends.'

'We are. Perhaps I'll see you in Austria later on. Where was it?'

'Oberwald. Come if you can. But why leave now? We're all going to be here at Malindi for another week.'

'I've had enough. I enjoyed the safari but I'm not sure I could stand a whole week on the beach, and anyway it's all rather spoiled now. It's better this way, Rowena.'

'If you insist. We *are* still friends, darling, aren't we?'

'Of course we are.'

'And you'll come to Oberwald?'

'We'll see.'

'I'll be at the Hotel Supercresta, the new one.'

'When?'

'Three and a half weeks, I think it is. I go straight from Nairobi.'

'What about clothes?'

'I'm travelling heavy, darling. I've got them with me.'

'Of course, you had it all planned didn't you? Well, we'll see. I'm leaving in a couple of hours. Write to me at home, Rowena.'

'Right. Incidentally I gave Jackie a piece of my mind *and* his marching orders. He's feeling sorry for himself this morning.'

'You didn't need to quarrel on my account. Nothing happened.'

'That wasn't *his* fault, was it?' Rowena smiled. 'I've taken care of him. I don't like alley cats.'

Caroline grinned as her breakfast arrived.

That evening in her hotel room in Nairobi she examined her luggage. Although most of her clothes were summer clothes, she had the warmer outfit in which she had left London. It would do. The idea of Oberwald appealed to her — not in three and a half weeks' time when the season had started, but now, at the end of November. She would be gone before Rowena and her friends arrived for their winter's ski-ing and general merry-making.

There was in fact no real reason for Caroline to go to Oberwald at all except that Rowena had put the name into her head. She merely wanted a couple of weeks by herself away from everyone, a quiet period after the fun of the safari and before settling in at Portcullis Manor for the winter.

She checked with the travel agency in the hotel. She could leave next day for Germany, spend a night at Munich and get to Oberwald quite easily the following day, after a three hour journey. She would have to make her own arrangements about a hotel when she got there. It sounded good enough.

She could buy a few clothes on the spot and meantime she wrote to Aunt Selina and told her her plans and asked her to get certain things from her room, parcel them up, and post them to her *post restante* at Oberwald post office. She hoped that would work. It wasn't a critical matter one way or the other.

Two days later she was booking in at the Rosengarten Hotel in Oberwald which, she had been assured, was small, quiet, intimate, with excellent food and a nice homely atmosphere. It was a typical Tyrolean village, small and apparently quiet, with wide-roofed houses, each with its balcony, standing above a lovely valley in the Kitzbuehel Alps. There was snow all round but not much had fallen yet on the village itself. She was assured that it would probably snow at any moment now. This did not particularly interest her one way or the other.

She registered, went to her room and unpacked, and then had lunch. Afterwards she bought some warm clothing

264

and read several brochures on the hotel, the village and the district. It seemed there was plenty to do — excursions could be made to Innsbruck, Salzburg and Kitzbuehel. She could go for walks or she could sit on the sun terrace. It wasn't exciting but it was all she wanted. She changed into a fancy woolly jumper and warm slacks, and a new pair of boots, and had tea in the small lounge. The proprietor was a friendly, plump Austrian who loved his job, and he was interested in this gold haired English girl on her own who had only booked in for two weeks and would leave before the ski-ing season began. The hotel was quiet and he speculated on her presence. He went over to speak to her.

'Is everything all right?' he asked in his friendly fashion. 'Your room is as you require?'

'Oh yes, thank you. I've done my shopping.'

'Good. What are your plans, may I ask?'

'Nothing at the moment. I'll explore the village tomorrow, and then I think the next day I'll go to Innsbruck. I've never been in Austria before.'

'Then we are honoured that you chose the Rosengarten.'

'What time is dinner?'

'An hour and a half.'

'I must go and write some letters first. I can post them here?'

'Just give them to me. I'll arrange everything.'

'Thank you very much Herr . . . '

'Wagele. Toni Wagele. Call me Toni. All the English visitors do.'

'Thank you Toni.'

'Ring if you want anything.'

'I will,' she promised.

He watched her go. A nice girl. So beautiful too, with that lovely hair and that smile. With a sigh for his own lost youth he went back to the desk just as the door opened and the tall broad-shouldered American came in.

'Good evening Herr Manisty.'

'Hullo Toni.'

'Did you ski?'

'Yes. At the top of Hochberg. It's not too bad. I want to get a little practice before the ski-ing really starts. How are things?'

'We have another guest.'

'Getting crowded, isn't it?' Magnus laughed.

'Ah but you will like this one. A beautiful woman.'

'That sounds exciting. I'm going to have a hot bath now.'

Toni Wagele looked after him sadly. Such a fine American young man and he hadn't even asked the girl's name. Young men weren't the same as they used to be. They weren't the same at all.

11

Magnus put on a white nylon ski shirt and pulled his heavy red and blue Fair Isle pullover over it. He combed his thick fair hair, and then left the room. He was hungry. He had had a strenuous day, walking all morning, and then going up to the top of Hochberg chair lift in the afternoon where he found some reasonable snow. He had skied a lot and he was out of condition. Tomorrow he would give it a miss — he would get on with his next book, and later in the afternoon he would walk in the village. He liked it. It was best just now, before the rush began. Oberwald was not one of the overcrowded spoiled resorts, but there was no doubt it was popular and in a few years he might not like it nearly so much. Meantime he enjoyed it.

He remembered his first time here.

He'd never skied outside of America before — indeed he had rarely skied outside of Vermont and New Hampshire. Somebody had recommended Toni Wagele and the Rosengarten, and he had spent three delightful weeks here during the month of February. That had been a good time. There had been a lot of good company that year, and the snow had been wonderful. Now they had a heated indoor swimming pool, and a new hotel. He didn't mind the change so long as it was within the bounds of reason. He went into the Keller Bar where Toni presided each evening, and ordered a Canada Dry ginger.

'Feeling better?' Toni asked. They were alone in the little rustic bar.

'Much. Where's everyone?'

'You're the first. We're going to be busy in two weeks' time.'

'I know, you warned me. I don't mind. I'll be ready to spend all my days ski-ing by then.'

'There are only six for dinner tonight.'

'Just a nice number, Toni. Make the most of it.' Magnus grinned. 'Of course your miserable heart will only rejoice when we are so crowded nobody can get near the bar and we have to sit so close at dinner, that we eat off one another's plates.'

'Now you know it isn't like that at the Rosengarten.'

'I was kidding. Where's this new girl?'

'Writing letters. No, here she is.'

The door opened and Caroline came in. She had not looked directly at Magnus. She had three letters in her hand and was smiling at Toni.

'Here you are Toni. Can I give them to you?'

'Certainly. What will you drink?'

'Something soft please.' She turned and looked at Magnus as she spoke, and froze. They stared at one another wordless.

'This is Herr Manisty,' Toni told her. 'An American. He was ski-ing today on the upper slopes. Fraulein Eaton from England.'

'I . . . um . . . er.' Magnus was stuck for words.

'You!' Caroline almost recoiled.

'Ah, you have met.'

'Yes,' Magnus said, still staring at Caroline. 'Miss Eaton and I met in England.'

'Then this is the reunion. We shall all have a drink — on Toni. What is it to be Fraulein?'

'Um . . . Tomato juice please.'

'Tomato juice? Have something stronger.'

'No thanks, I don't drink.'

'Ha, then you are like Herr Manisty. More Canada Dry?'

Magnus nodded.

'I didn't know you were here,' Caroline said suddenly. 'I heard you were in Austria, but I didn't know it was here.'

'I thought you were in Kenya.'

'I was. I left early. Somebody recommended Oberwald and I thought I would have a quiet time before the ski-ing started.'

'I see.' The drinks were served.

'Thanks Toni. Cheers Caroline.'

They all raised their glasses and drank.

'You did not know about one another?' Toni asked, interested.

They shook their heads. 'No,' Caroline said. 'We didn't know.'

'This is good luck then. You should learn to ski now. Perhaps Herr Manisty . . . '

'I don't want to ski,' Caroline said loudly. 'I came here for quiet — and peace,' she added meaningly.

'Here's to peace.' Magnus raised his glass. 'I'm all for it myself.'

'I'm relieved to hear it.'

'I'm busy most of the time,' Magnus went on. 'Either writing or ski-ing.'

'Are you writing another book?'

'Making notes. I'll write it when I go back at Easter. I have to give up that cottage, you see, and move all my things somewhere else. It's getting expensive.'

'Oh.'

'Then there's the restaurant. They'll

be starting to do all the alterations in April. I must be back for that.'

'I came here to walk and explore the region.'

'I shan't be troubling you much,' Magnus informed her.

Toni was listening, puzzled. What was wrong with them? They were so formal, so polite, and spoke so mysteriously.

They kept up their stiff formality all through dinner and after, until Caroline went off to bed. Magnus sat in the bar and had a final Canada Dry which he didn't really want but which was an excuse to sit and talk to Toni. He did not refer to Caroline and at last he too went to his room. Next morning he decided to go into breakfast early, have a cup of coffee, and clear off for the day. He would ski again. It would keep him out of the hotel. Caroline had the same idea. She did not want to meet him at breakfast either, so she too went down early and of course they met.

'Er . . . hullo.' He nodded abruptly.
'Good morning.'

They stirred coffee in silence.

'Sleep well?' he asked.

'Very.'

'The mountain air,' he said cryptically. 'I must go.'

'Magnus.'

'Yes?'

'I can move.'

'Please don't move on my account. I don't expect we shall see each other often and there are other people to talk to.'

'Quite. But Magnus . . . '

'Yes.'

'I didn't mean to be quite so rude. You don't understand.'

'It doesn't matter. Whether you call me piglet or a filthy swine is not important if you happen to be a Jew who hates pork.'

With this somewhat involved remark he got up and stalked out, leaving her biting her lip. She wanted to undo some of the harm. She had been forceful. She could not remember her words, but she knew she had been pretty bitter in her condemnation. Oh well, obviously he wanted to forget it. Perhaps that was better. She lingered over the coffee and then had more and some hot rolls with the second cup. There was no hurry now.

For three days they did little but exchange brief, formal greetings, for all the world like two uncongenial strangers who wished to do nothing but give each other a wide berth. Caroline went to Salzburg and to Innsbruck, while Magnus haunted the higher slopes looking for decent ski-ing. There were always good runs round Oberwald, even this early, if you looked for them. He could not concentrate on his book at all, with Caroline so close, so he did not even try. Anyway there was no hurry about it.

On the fourth day Caroline's parcel arrived together with an ecstatic letter from Aunt Selina telling her that (guess what?) Magnus was also at the Rosengarten Hotel in Oberwald and hadn't it been a surprise meeting him?

Some surprise, Caroline thought as she put away jumpers, warm under-wear, and thick socks. By now she had bought so much that she hardly needed the extra clothing. She was still undecided about moving out of the hotel. It would be better if she did, but how to explain it to the charming and hospitable Toni? It seemed a pity to penalise him for what had nothing to do with him.

'Why don't you go for a moonlight sleigh ride?' Toni asked.

'Can I?'

'Yes of course. I can arrange it. Tomorrow night?'

'All right.'

'What about your friend Herr Man-isty? It would be nice for you to have company.'

'No thank you,' Caroline said stiffly.

'Sorry.' He apologised but he did not know quite for what. 'You are not such good friends perhaps?'

'Not very. Not *close* friends.'

'I see.' It was sad, Toni mused. Very

sad. It would be nice if they had a wedding here in the village, but of course things like that did not happen. They were just good friends, which was the peculiar English way of saying *not* very good friends. An odd, contradictory race.

When Magnus returned he stopped for a drink before going for his bath. Caroline was already in the bar. Toni greeted him with a wide grin.

'You are late. A parcel came for you. Here.'

He produced a small flat parcel along with the inevitable Canada Dry, and Magnus examined the postmark.

'From home,' he said, wondering what it was.

'Open it,' Toni grinned.

Magnus smiled back and undid the string. It was a book of some sort. Inside was a brief note from his mother.

'A present?' Toni asked.

'Yes, from my mother.' He was taking tissue paper from the small, leather bound volume with gold leaf on the front, and a card.

'Ah, is it your birthday?' Toni demanded.

'As a matter of fact, it is. I'd forgotten.'

'Then we will have a party. How is it, happy returns?'

'Thank you Toni.'

'Many happy returns, Magnus,' Caroline murmured.

'Thank you Caroline.'

While Toni was announcing to the other people in the bar that it was Magnus's birthday and that drinks were on the house, Magnus was staring at his book.

'What is it?' Caroline could not resist asking.

'Oh, a book I like. I've always liked it. My mother must have remembered that I lost my copy. It's nicely bound. A library edition.'

'What is it? What's it about?'

'You wouldn't have heard of it. It's a classic.'

'I like the classics.'

'You don't know,' he grinned and

held it out. She read the title. *A New England Girlhood*, by Lucy Larcom.

'I haven't heard of it,' she admitted.

'It's my favourite reading. It takes me back to another century when life was much nicer and simpler. You'd have to be born in New England to understand its appeal.'

'I see. It's an old book is it?'

'Written in 1889, but it's an autobiography and she was born in 1824 at a place called Beverly in Massachusetts. She was born only nine years after the Battle of Waterloo and when she died the technological revolution had actually started although nobody knew it at the time. It's not everybody's cup of tea but it's my bedside book, especially now that I'm away from home.'

'I see. It sounds nice.'

'It's quaint and very unfashionable. I'm not very fashionable myself, sometimes.'

He flicked open the covers at the last pages and searched. 'Listen to this,' he said. ''I have always regarded it as a better ambition to be a true woman than to become a successful writer. To be the second would never have seemed to me desirable, without also being the first.' I wonder what the women's lib ladies would make of Lucy Larcom. And this. 'Education is growth, the development of our best possibilities from within outward; and it cannot be carried on as it should be except in a school, just such a school as we all find ourselves in — this world of human beings by whom we are surrounded!' I wonder if any of the militant student leaders have read that. Of course,' he shrugged, 'that's only by the way. The book really is about life in New England. That's the appeal.'

Toni interrupted at that point, for it was a birthday and no time for a tête à tête. Caroline was rather sorry. For just a few minutes he had opened up a little. She would love to get her hands on his book and read it for herself.

★   ★   ★

They had quite a small private celebration that night in the Keller Bar, some seven or eight of them, together with Toni and his wife Trudi. It was quite late when they finished and Magnus felt he was awash with ginger ale. He had intended to hold out the olive branch and suggest to Caroline that next day they visit Rattenberg, but she went up to her room early, while he was involved in a discussion with someone, and so he missed the chance. He decided to ask her in the morning.

He would have been surprised if he could have seen Caroline in her room, for she lay on her bed, feeling miserable, tears welling in her eyes. Suddenly she knew very clearly that she desperately wanted him, yet the whole evening had made her conscious of the fact that she had no part in his life. He had been polite, certainly, but he paid hardly any attention to her. She did not blame him. She felt unhappy and frustrated.

Next morning she said she had a

headache and had some coffee sent up to her room. Magnus hung about for a time but she did not come out so in the end he decided to ski again. There had been more snow. He decided to go for a day's rambling in the snow. It was a different sort of exercise, and it was a fine bright day for it. He took a packed lunch and set off.

Caroline came down at lunch time, feeling a little more cheerful. She had got over her mood of black depression. If she couldn't have Magnus, she couldn't and there was no point in going on mourning over the fact. She visited the skating rink after lunch and spent the afternoon there. In the evening she changed into warm clothing for she was going out for her sleigh ride later on after dinner.

'Where's Mr. Manisty?' she asked Toni.

'I don't know. He's very late. He must have stopped off somewhere in the village.'

'Has he been ski-ing?'

'Yes, not on the slopes but rambling. He took a lunch with him.'

'Perhaps I ought to learn after all.'

'Why not stay then?'

'We'll see,' she smiled.

They talked for a time about her safari holiday in Kenya and then Toni began to look worried.

'I wish Mr. Manisty would come in,' he complained. 'He should know better than to alarm us like this.'

Dinner came and went and no Magnus came. By now Toni was seriously alarmed.

'There must have been an accident,' he said.

'Are you sure?'

'I'll find out. I've sent for my brother's son and he will go round the whole village for me.'

'Suppose he doesn't find Magnus?'

'Then he's up there somewhere.'

'What happens?'

'We are organised for these things but people don't often go missing quite like this. I will tell various people and first thing in the morning they will start a search. I don't even know which lift he was on, or which direction he took.'

'Tomorrow? You mean he'd be up on the mountain all night?'

'What can one do in the dark?' Toni asked. 'We'll soon know if he is safe or not.'

'But it might snow.'

'It *will* snow. It probably is snowing now, higher up. It will snow here tonight.'

'What will he do?'

'Who can say? It depends where he is and if he is injured.'

'Injured? He may just be lost.'

'I doubt it. Mr. Manisty is not a man who loses himself. He must have had an accident.'

Caroline's heart sank. She did not like this at all. Within the hour they all knew that Magnus was nowhere in the village. A search was organised for first thing in the morning and it was discovered that he had gone up on the drag lift which was in use, but had not been seen since.

'Where would he go from there?' Toni wondered. 'It is very odd. I would not expect him to go very far.'

Caroline cancelled her sleigh ride. She was in no mood for the beauties of Oberwald by moonlight. Instead she stayed talking to Toni in the vague hope that something would happen, that by some miracle Magnus would return.

But he did not. In the end she went to bed and lay awake most of the night. She was suddenly very afraid.

12

The inevitable happened. At about four-thirty in the morning Caroline fell into a heavy sleep and did not waken up till after ten-thirty. She dressed hurriedly and looked for Toni who was speaking on the telephone. He hung up, saw her and smiled.

'What's happening?' she asked. 'What is the news?'

'Of Herr Manisty? No news. They are searching.'

'I wanted to go too.'

'You couldn't,' he laughed. 'Only an accomplished skier could do that. They'll find him, and soon I expect.'

'Are there any dangerous places up there?' she asked gesturing vaguely. She knew nothing about the mountains and the snow, or about ski-ing.

'It depends what you mean by dangerous. Herr Manisty is a very experienced skier and he would do nothing stupid. Of course anyone can break a leg and it might be as simple as that. The most experienced skier could do it under certain circumstances, you see.'

She did not fully see but she nodded.

'There are no proper danger spots, no ravines or anything. Not unless he has gone far into the mountains and he would not do that. He was quite late in leaving here. He can't have gone too far. They'll find him.'

It was all very well saying that they would find him, she thought, but in what condition? Alive or . . . ? She shied away from the alternative. The rest of the morning simply dragged past. Every time she looked at her wristwatch it seemed that the hands had not moved at all. She was in a state of nervous exhaustion when Toni suggested a light lunch. She refused to go out into the village. She was compelled to remain where she was, waiting. It was mid afternoon when they brought him back on a stretcher, covered with bankets. There was a young doctor with him and Caroline stood petrified, frightened out of her wits, as they brought him through the doors and carried him upstairs. He lay still, an inert mound under the dark blankets, as though he were already dead.

'What's happened?' she asked Toni frantically. 'Find out how he is, Toni.'

'All right, all right. You'd better have a drink.'

'No thanks. Ask how he is.'

'They must have time. The doctor will be back soon to tell me. Patience, fraulein.'

Patience, she thought wildly. What a time to talk about patience. She was consumed with impatience. After what seemed like hours the doctor came back and entered into a long conversation with Toni, not a word of which Caroline understood. She thought she would go mad with frustration, until at last the doctor had done. Toni spoke rapidly to Trudi who hurried away.

Caroline grabbed his arm.

'Tell me!'

'I'm sorry. He hurt his foot. He cannot walk. He spent all night in a snowdrift. They only found him by accident.'

'How *serious* is it?'

'He'll be all right. He's frozen stiff and it is lucky he did not freeze to death, but he managed to keep warm enough. Two days in bed, plenty of hot soup, some injections, and he will be as good as new. There is no need to worry. It was his foot. He couldn't get back, and he was caught in the snowstorm up there. He wasn't far from the lift when it happened, but far enough. Don't worry.'

She suddenly went limp.

'No,' she said dully. 'Do you know, perhaps I will have a drink. What do you recommend?'

'For you? Brandy. Wait.'

He brought her a large brandy and she drank it, making a face as she did so.

'Ugh. Do people actually do that for fun?'

'You'll feel better in a moment.'

It was true. She did begin to feel a little warm glow. She left him, for he had things to attend to, and she went and sat out on the sun terrace, staring at the white-clad slopes all round. It was lovely. She could see the whole village and the church with its lovely slender pointed spire. It was a nice place.

She made up her mind quickly. It was time to go home. Magnus Manisty meant far too much to her. She did not ever want to live through another night like last night, haunted by the fear that he might be dead, or at best seriously injured.

When she told Toni he was amazed, but she was insistent so he helped her to arrange her journey, which was easy at that particular time, and promised to have her bill ready next morning.

'We shall miss you,' he said. 'What am I to say to Mr. Manisty when he asks me about you?'

'If he does ask, just say I went home,' she said lightly, putting a bold face on things. 'That's where I'm going. Home in time for Christmas.'

'You were going to stay another week.'

'I know, but I miss home.'

'I understand.'

She left the following day, while Magnus lay in bed recovering. He spent all that day and the following one in his room, limping down to the bar on the second night, a little shaky still but otherwise well. They all joked with him about it, making light of it. Magnus entered into the spirit of the thing. It was very good to be alive. He'd had a bit of a scare himself although he had not been too worried in the beginning. He would not like to spend a night out on the mountain again.

Suddenly he turned to Toni.

'Where's Caroline?'

'She went home.'

'Home? To England? When?'

'Yesterday, while you were in bed resting.'

'But I thought she was staying longer.'

'She changed her mind. She said she missed home.'

'Oh.' He looked round the bar disconsolately, no longer quite so exuberant at being with these friendly pleasant people again. 'Well.' He looked up and saw the understanding in Toni's eyes. He grinned. 'Perhaps I ought to go too, Toni, and come back later.'

'I think perhaps you should. Don't worry about the room. I'll have no trouble finding someone to take your place. It's going to be a good season.'

'Thanks. I'll go in a few days.'

Toni sighed. It was really too bad. They had become his favourite customers. That was what came of having favourites. Be polite, be friendly, make them welcome, but never, never become involved. His brother had told him that a long time ago, and now he realised how true it was.

★　★　★

Caroline finished her shopping and went to The Spinnaker for coffee. She put down her shopping basket, took off her gloves, and ran a hand through her hair. It was a cold dull day, and she wore a warm tweed suit and a thick blue jumper under the coat. She ordered coffee and hot buttered toast, and then opened the morning newspaper and glanced at the headlines.

It would soon be Christmas, she thought. She wondered for a fleeting moment how Magnus was in Austria. He'd be fully recovered now, maybe even ski-ing again if his ankle and foot were better, probably looking forward very much to Christmas with Toni. Well, it was all a long way from Walton and no longer quite real. She would spend Christmas at Portcullis which was something she always liked. They usually celebrated it quietly, going to the midnight service on Christmas Eve, and then getting up for a late breakfast on Christmas Day, opening presents at the breakfast table.

Aunt Selina had been very sweet ever since she came home, much to Caroline's amusement. Obviously Aunt Selina thought that she and Magnus had some sort of understanding. Poor Aunt Selina. She would be disappointed at Easter when she, Caroline, went off again.

The coffee and toast arrived and she was pouring when she was aware of somebody sitting down opposite her. She felt a twinge of annoyance. There were vacant tables. She finished pouring before looking up and then her jaw dropped. Magnus, in a heavy sweater over a turtle necked jumper, looking for all the world as though he had just come off the *piste*, was grinning at her.

'Hullo, mind if I join you?'

'No.' She blinked. 'I thought you were in Austria.'

'I was. I'm not.' He grinned more widely and ordered coffee and toast for himself. 'When I heard you'd gone I decided I didn't want to stay either.'

'Why not?' she asked suspiciously.

'That's a good question.'

'Are you all right now?' she asked changing the subject.

'Yes. I'm fine. It was a mild sprain and kept me limping for about six days.'

'How did you know I was here?' she asked puzzled.

'I didn't. I rang your father about twenty-five minutes ago and he said you were out shopping and invited me to lunch. I accepted. Then I came out to buy a couple of things, didn't see you anywhere, and decided to come in here. I was pleasantly surprised to find you.'

'You're coming to lunch?' She did not know if she was pleased.

'Yes. Do you mind?'

'No, why should I mind?'

'I don't know. You pushed off from Oberwald very suddenly and without warning. I thought I might be getting on your nerves.'

'It wasn't that.'

'I'm glad.'

'In fact . . . well, I felt pretty awful when I heard you were missing.'

'So did I, when I found myself stuck on the slopes,' he laughed.

'I meant . . . '

'I know what you meant.' He put a hand over hers. 'You were worried, weren't you?'

'Yes. How did you know?'

'Toni told me. I don't know why you were — I thought I rated pretty low in your book — but I do know you were.'

'I was frantic. I thought I'd die of fright.'

'Because of me? Do you know something, all that awful night I kept thinking about you and when it got really bad and I became a little bit afraid — you know, one does get scared no matter how big-headed — I kept thinking one thing. She'll never know how much I love her. I kept thinking it over and over and over, till I almost became dizzy.'

'*Magnus!*'

'What happened Caroline? What went wrong?'

'It was so silly. I don't know how to tell you.'

'Try me.'

'I found you and Lisette kissing like mad, eating one another almost.'

'Huh? Lisette and me? You can't have done.'

'I did. I opened the sitting-room door and there you were, like Romeo and Juliet with a happy ending.'

'I never did . . . ' His voice trailed away as memory returned. 'Oh that. Oh lord, that wasn't what you think. It was a sort of celebratory kiss. She'd just succeeded in persuading Richard that he didn't want you after all. He was going to break it to you gently. After all, we were old friends Caroline. I certainly wasn't eating her.' She was eating him, he thought. Lisette was always enthusiastic about whatever she did.

'I guessed afterwards that whatever it was, it wasn't what I had imagined. I was in love with you. It was awful. I was furious. I thought you'd been pulling my leg saying all the nice things you had.'

'Me? Pull your leg? Oh Caroline.'

'I saw you and Lisette. It looked *awful*. I felt — I can't tell you how I felt.'

'When you told me off the way you did, I felt pretty bad too. Think of all the time we've wasted. Caroline do you really love me?'

'I've never loved anyone else. But no more nonsense going off on your own like that and hurting your ankle.'

'Then you must learn to ski and come with me in future. Not to Austria. To Vermont. You'll want to visit your father- and mother-in-law every year.'

She gave him a smile that blinded him.

Two waitresses were standing at the counter when one stiffened.

'Look at that, Elsie,' she hissed.

'What?'

'Over there. In public and in broad

298

daylight. I never.'

Elsie looked. She never, either. It looked fun though. She rather wished she did.

THE END

Other titles in the
Linford Romance Library:

PHOENIX IN THE ASHES

Georgina Ferrand

Paul Varonne had been dead for six months, yet at Château Varonne reminders of him were still evident. Living there was his mother, who still believed him alive and Chantal, his amoral cousin. Into this brooding atmosphere comes Paul's widow, Francesca, after a nervous breakdown. When she meets Peter Devlin, an Englishman staying in the village, it seems that happiness is within her grasp — until she learns the staggering truth about the château and its inhabitants.

NEVER LOOK BACK

Janet Roscoe

Nina, anxious to save her marriage to Charles, wants to stop the rot before it's too late. Charles, refusing to admit that there is anything wrong, tells Nina to stop imagining problems. But there is her step-brother, Duncan Stevens — easy-going and artistic, everything that Charles is not . . . Charles' sister-in-law likens divorce to a mere game of chess — yet the effect of a tragic death, seven years previously, triggers off a happening of such magnitude that Nina faces the truth at last.

PASSPORT TO FEAR

Patricia Hutchinson

Rose and Ray, two young women travelling by ship from India to England are alike in appearance. Both orphans, Ray is wealthy, while Rose has lived on her wits. Ray has a heart condition and is going to England to her guardian. But then when she dies Rose takes on the other girl's identity. However, in England Rose becomes a victim of her new guardian's greed and her life is threatened. Can she yet find love and happiness?

SMILE OF A STRANGER

Mavis Thomas

When Ruth Stafford joins her mother at the Sea Winds Hotel, she has misgivings about Cecily Stafford's imminent marriage to Willard Enderby. Ruth suspects he has designs on her mother's recent legacy. If so, she is determined to unmask him! She is helped by another hotel guest, and finds herself falling deeply in love with him . . . but is this endearing stranger any more trustworthy than Willard? Joys, heartbreaks and divided loyalties lie ahead before her questions find answers.